ONCE WICKED

Teas & Temptations Cozy Mysteries
Book One

CINDY STARK

www.cindystark.com

Once Wicked © 2018 C. Nielsen

Cover Design by Kelli Ann Morgan
Inspire Creative Services

License Notes

Welcome to Stonebridge, Massachusetts

Welcome to Stonebridge, a small town in Massachusetts where the label "witch" is just as dangerous now as it was in 1692. From a distance, most would say the folks in Stonebridge are about the friendliest around. But a dark and disturbing history is the backbone that continues to haunt citizens of this quaint town where many have secrets they never intend to reveal.

Visit www.cindystark.com for more titles and release information. Sign up for Cindy's newsletter to ensure you're always hearing the latest happenings.

PROLOGUE

Stonebridge, Massachusetts 1680

Clarabelle Foster stood next to a wooden work table and stared in amazement as her mother's delicate hands crushed dried flowers and leaves with a pestle. She sniffed, enjoying the scents that rose to greet her.

"How do you know which flowers to pick, mama?" Most of them smelled good and were pretty. Except the nettles. She didn't like those.

Her mother smiled gently at her. "Well, you pick the ones that are right for the job. We're going to turn these into a salve that will heal yours and papa's cuts when you get hurt."

Clarabelle nodded, her eyes wide. "You're the best at making magic."

Her mom gasped and dropped the pestle. It landed on the wood with a resounding thud. She pressed her fingertips over Clarabelle's mouth. "*Clarabelle.* Where on earth did you hear that word?"

She didn't understand why her mother was so worried. "Magic?" she said beneath her mama's fingers. "Genevieve said that's what you do. Her mama, too. And her mama doesn't care if she says it. She can say witch, too."

Her mother's jaw dropped, and worry creased her forehead. "No, no, no. I've told you before there are some words too dangerous to say."

She shrugged, not understanding why her mother made a big fuss. "It's just a word, Mama."

A cloud of worry surrounded her mother, reaching out toward Clarabelle with sticky fingers. The feelings made her tummy hurt, and she tried to avoid them by taking a step back from the work table.

"It's not just a word," her mother said in hushed anger. "If you say that to the wrong person, they will come after our family. Is that what you want? To have us torn apart? They would shun your father and likely kill me. They might hurt you, too. *Is that what you want?*"

Shameful tears welled in her eyes. "No, mama. I don't want you to die. I don't want any of us to die. I just want to stay here with you and papa."

Her mother grasped her chin and tilted her face upward. A stern expression darkened her features. "Then don't ever speak those words again. *Do...you...understand?*"

She didn't like this side of her mother. It frightened her. "Yes, Mama. I understand."

Her mother exhaled a breath, and her relief was a soothing balm to Clarabelle. "Good. Let's get back to this lesson. What do we call these purple flowers?"

"Lavender, Mama. And that other one is mint."

"Smart girl. Keep listening to me and not your friends, and we will all be just fine."

Her mother might have said the words, but she could tell she still worried. And Clarabelle didn't want to worry her mother. Next time she saw Genevieve, she'd tell her what she thought of her stupid words.

CHAPTER ONE

Current Day

Hazel Hardy's thighs burned as she pedaled her bicycle up the incline toward the big Victorian manor at the top of the hill.

She'd pulled her auburn hair into a ponytail to keep the loose curls out of her face while she rode. Between jeans and her favorite olive-green sweater, along with the exercise, she'd stay warm enough. It was only mid-March, and the days could still carry a chill. Luckily, this year, they'd been blessed with unseasonably warm weather and the sun was out today, bright and warm, so she'd be just fine.

She'd tucked tins of her handcrafted teas in the bike's basket, and they bumped against each other with each pedal, clanging out a metallic tune. She couldn't picture a more beautiful small town than Stonebridge, Massachusetts, with its tree-lined streets coursing between a mixture of newer buildings and centuries-old rock-hewn churches. For an earth witch, it was perfect.

No matter where Hazel went, she always found a smiling face. Her mom had missed the mark completely when she'd warned her a few months back about the town that still harbored hatred against witches going on three hundred years.

But Hazel had yearned to learn more about her heritage, and the people she'd met in Stonebridge were as nice as sweetened chamomile tea at bedtime. The cherry on top was that she'd never have to see Victor's cheating face again.

Filling her lungs repeatedly to compensate for her thumping heart, she gave a last burst of energy to wheel up the Winthrop's driveway. Hopefully all this biking would compensate for her obsession with cherry macaroons and hazelnut cannoli.

A loud horn battered her eardrums from behind, sending her into a panic. She turned the handlebars to the right in a quick, knee-jerk reaction to avoid the threat. Her front tire slid sideways as she struggled to keep her bike upright. She wobbled to the left and teetered to the right.

When her front tire hit soft gravel off the edge of the driveway, her bike launched her like an angry bull did a novice cowboy.

The palms of her hands took the brunt of the landing. She skidded for a moment before rolling to a stop.

Unladylike curses hovered on her tongue, and she swiveled her head, ready to unleash her rage.

Overweight, gray-haired, and full of himself, Winston Winthrop didn't spare her a glance as he drove his black Mercedes past her and parked between the sparkling fountain and elegant house.

Hazel struggled to catch a decent breath as she got to her feet. She wiped her dusty, scraped up palms on her jeans.

Across the drive, Winthrop's manservant dashed from the house to open his employer's car door.

Up until this point, Hazel hadn't come face-to-face with her client's husband. But she was about to now. She'd heard rumors of the self-important, rude man, but she'd had a hard time believing such a man could be married to the sweet and gentle Mrs. Winthrop.

Apparently, she'd been wrong.

Hazel hobbled to where her bike had fallen after her spectacular dismount, and she lifted it from the ground, inspecting it for damage. Lucky for Mr. Winthrop, her favorite mode of transportation remained intact. She picked up the tin boxes of tea and placed them in the basket, grateful they'd survived as well.

She strode toward the house, walking as fast as her tender knees would allow.

As she approached, the wealthy aristocrat dropped his keys into the hands of his employee. "Do take care to keep the drive clear, Mick. We wouldn't want anyone to get hurt."

Hazel opened her mouth to give Mr. Winthrop the verbal lashing he deserved, but Mick shook his head in warning, a lock of the twenty-something man's dark hair falling into his eyes.

Mr. Winthrop walked toward the house, exuding a privileged air. "And do get yourself a haircut," he called over his shoulder. "We've had enough trouble with witches and beggars in the past. I can't continue to employ anyone looking so unkempt."

Hazel clenched her jaw. *"Witches and beggars?"* She spat out the offensive words to Mick. If she could make one wish, she'd hope never to encounter the nasty man again.

She'd never tell her mother she'd been right about the residents of Stonebridge who still believed those who practiced witchcraft were spawns of Satan, a notion some residents had passed down for generations, since the early colonization of the area. Up until this moment, she hadn't witnessed evidence of such despicable and unfounded attitudes toward others, and even now, her heart didn't want to believe it was true.

Witches were not the devil's disciples, and she took issue with anyone who thought they were. Honoring Mother Earth and her gifts was anything but evil.

If there was a rotten egg in the bunch, it was Mr. Winthrop.

Mick cast a wary glance toward the house and then switched his dark gaze back to Hazel. "Ignore him. He's an old man out of touch with reality."

She liked Mick Ramsey, though she couldn't get a clear reading from his soul. He had many emotional walls, though that alone didn't make him bad. Sometimes people erected barriers to hide something. Other times, their walls were for protection.

She liked to think it was the latter, and he just needed a friend.

Hazel snorted. "I'd like to show him reality."

"Wouldn't we all?" Mick countered.

She considered her options. A healthy dose of the itches...in a very uncomfortable place? A potion that would leave his stomach heaving? The thought of Mr. Winthrop trying discreetly to take care of his issues brought a smile back to her face.

Mick nodded to the white woven basket on the front of her pink bike. "Tea for Mrs. Winthrop?"

She smiled, grateful to focus on something else. "Every Monday. Speaking of which, I'd better hurry. I'm already behind, and the matron of the kitchen, as I like to call her, gets snippy when she has to wait for me."

He laughed and shook his head. "That's one woman I try to avoid at all costs."

"Mrs. Jones isn't that bad," Hazel said, and they both laughed because they knew she was. "Catch you later."

She parked her bicycle alongside the garage and retrieved one of several tins from the woven basket. With her delivery safe in her tenderized hands, she followed the flat stone path around the side of the elaborate home to the back door where she didn't bother to knock.

"Hello?" she called as she entered, and immediately Mrs. Jones, the curmudgeonly cook appeared from inside the pantry.

"Good morning, Hazel." Mrs. Jones graced her with a never-before-seen smile that surprised her.

She took a few seconds to recover from the shock. "Good morning to you, too. You seem particularly happy today." Perhaps she'd misjudged her. After all, working for Mr. Winthrop could make anyone ornery.

Mrs. Jones widened her eyes as though also surprised, and the bright aura hovering around her dimmed. "Nonsense. I'm no happier than any other day."

Hazel stared at her for a long moment, sad that the woman had chosen to return to unhappiness. She sighed and held up the tin. "I have Mrs. Winthrop's tea delivery."

Mrs. Jones jerked her head toward the stove. "Her tea service is ready to go. Just waiting on you. I've been keeping the water hot for the past fifteen minutes."

And, just like that, the waspish old woman was back. "Sorry. I stopped at June Porter's first, and she can...well, you know..." How did she say this without being rude? "She likes her conversation."

The cook grunted. "Best keep your hands on your ears when she's around, or she'll talk them off before she sends you on your way."

Hazel smiled in agreement and headed toward the tea service Mrs. Jones had prepared. She could have mentioned her unfortunate incident outside, but she doubted she'd gain any sympathy. "I'll just wash my hands and head on up."

She hesitated for a moment, reluctant to ask her question. "Shall I put away the remaining tea?"

Mrs. Jones lifted a sarcastic brow. "Does anyone touch anything in my kitchen? Ever?"

"No." Hazel answered, the same as she had the other four weeks she'd been delivering tea. It seemed wrong to leave it for Mrs. Jones, but the woman barely tolerated Hazel as it was. Hazel quickly finished her task and headed for the elaborate staircase with the mahogany handrail and turned balusters that she loved so much.

The home Hazel had rented was older as well and had retained an air of history with arched doorways and decorative moulding between the ceiling and walls. But where her house was akin to a common person, Mrs. Winthrop's was the grand lady of the town, and Hazel never tired of visiting.

When Hazel's new assistant at her shop, Hazel's Teas and Temptations, had suggested door-to-door service to increase her customer base and therefore revenue, Hazel had questioned her sanity. People wanted pizza delivered, not tea.

But Gretta had been right to an extent. Many of the fifty and older crowd of ladies of Stonebridge loved the idea of gourmet tea being delivered straight to their doors, especially when they learned Mrs. Winthrop had signed up for the service. Most of these women came from prominent families who had lived in Massachusetts since colonial times, and they had the money to show for it.

Mrs. Winthrop's influence had sent Hazel's bottom line sailing into the black, and she couldn't be more grateful.

Which was why she'd agreed to also serve a pot of her gourmet tea every Monday to Mrs. Winthrop, allowing time for lovely conversation with a woman who rarely left her house. It was the least Hazel could do to show her gratitude, and besides, she'd found she enjoyed their time together, too.

The stairs of the old house creaked as Hazel ascended, a sentry of sorts, announcing her arrival. Hazel followed the now-familiar path she always took to the end of the hall and then knocked on the last door on the left.

"Come in," Mrs. Winthrop said.

Hazel balanced the tray on one hand and turned the doorknob.

Inside, sixty-nine-year-old Florence Winthrop sat at a Victorian dressing table with several bottles of nail polish in front of her. Patterned gold on ivory walls were the backdrop for the elegantly carved mahogany bed that dominated the room, complete with a gorgeous dusty rose quilt that matched the color of the curtains.

"Good morning, Mrs. Winthrop." Hazel made her way to the small table and two chairs near the window where they always drank tea. She lowered the tray that also carried some delicious-looking blueberry scones and Florence's joint supplements to the table and turned back to her client.

The frail woman graced her with a smile. "Good morning to you, my dear, and, please, call me Florence. We've known each other long enough and calling me Mrs. Winthrop makes me feel old."

"Of course." Hazel gave her an approving nod. "I'm glad to see you're up and out of bed early this morning."

Some days, Mrs. Winthrop, make that Florence, had still been asleep when she'd arrived. Her ailments, whatever they were, tired the poor woman something fierce and added a good ten years to her looks though she really wasn't that old at all.

Florence graced her with a smile. "Today is a good day. Hardly any pain at all."

"I'm so happy to hear that." Hazel found it difficult not to add a little something to her tea to help with those aches and pains, but she'd promised her mother she'd not use any potions or spells whilst in Stonebridge.

The whole idea that she'd had to promise to her mother seemed silly, but the town had a history of murdering innocent witches. Long ago, her ancestors had run in the middle of the night to escape persecution.

Times had changed, but, apparently not as much as she would have expected.

Hazel moved to the dressing table and inspected the array of nail polish. "Looks like you're planning to get dressed up. Is Mr. Winthrop taking you out on the town?"

Florence snorted and shook her head. "No, nothing special. Albert and I haven't dated in years." She shrugged. "I just wanted to do something small to feel pretty."

She met Hazel's gaze with a sad one of her own. "I haven't felt pretty in so long. If only I could be young again like you and Rachel."

Hazel gave her a kind smile. "You're a very beautiful woman, Florence. Rachel and I don't have anything on you." Though Hazel also envied the Winthrop maid's figure. She wouldn't mind having her sleek blond hair, too, as opposed to her own unruly auburn curls that tended to get out of hand at times.

Mrs. Winthrop stood and placed a hand on the dressing table to steady herself. "You have your youth, and that's what men want. That's what we all want."

She linked her arm through Mrs. Winthrop's and led her to the tea table.

"Be a dear and bring the polish, too, won't you? Perhaps you can help me paint my nails after we've had tea."

Hazel returned and scooped up the six different bottles of polish. One by one, she set them along the side of the tea table before she took her seat. Her so-called tea delivery service had become more of a social service, but she didn't mind. The ladies in town who chose that service appreciated the company and didn't mind paying extra for Hazel's time.

Plus, as her assistant, Gretta, suggested, it was a great way to get to know the town's residents and ingratiate herself with them.

"I brought a new flavor today," Hazel said as she set a tea strainer in Florence's cup. "It's a strawberry green tea blend."

The older woman lifted the teacup and held it near her nose. "That smells divine, Hazel. Do I detect traces of grapefruit in there?"

"Nose of a bloodhound," she said with a smile. "No one could get anything past you."

Florence winked and touched the tip of her nose. "Not to say that they haven't tried."

"A fool's errand," she said, and they both chuckled.

Hazel poured hot water into both of their cups and picked up a bottle of light pink polish while the tea leaves steeped. "This is a lovely color. May I?"

"Certainly. We should both paint our nails before you leave."

Hazel opened the bottle and drew the brush across one of her nails, leaving a lovely shade of pink in its path. "So pretty."

Florence agreed.

After they'd finished their tea and blueberry scones that Mrs. Jones had provided for them, Florence lifted a bottle of cherry red polish. "I think I should like this color."

Hazel let out a low whistle and grinned. "Perfect for a sexy siren like yourself."

Florence blushed bright pink. "Stop, young lady. You'll embarrass me."

"All right." Hazel didn't want to tease her too much. "Give me your hand."

The older woman spread a napkin over the gleaming wooden table and laid her hand out, palm down. With careful, precise strokes, Hazel painted bright red on each of the woman's nails.

When she finished, she set back with a smile. "Gorgeous."

A smile crept across Florence's face. "I used to wear this shade all the time when I was younger, back before this damned disease crippled me."

Hazel yearned to tell her how sorry she was that she'd been afflicted as she had, but that would help nothing. "Any time you want me to paint them, just ask." She lifted a bottle of clear polish. "How about a top coat so your color will last longer?"

The woman rolled her eyes and shook her head. "Not that one. It works a little too well."

Hazel laughed. "How can it work too well?"

"It stays on even after you want it to come off. I don't want red nails forever." She pushed the clear coat aside. "Use the other one."

"I understand completely. I once had a beautiful shade of gold polish with flecks of glitter in it. I used tons of cotton balls soaked with polish remover before I could get it off. Such a pain."

"Exactly." The older woman agreed with a firm nod of her head.

Hazel selected a second bottle of top coat and applied it to the woman's nails. "There. You look like you've just come from the beauty salon."

She beamed as she examined her hands. "I do. Wait until Albert sees. Now, finish your nails before you need to leave."

"Yes—"

A terrified scream for help cut her short. Her gaze flew to Florence's. "Someone's hurt."

Color drained from the older woman's face as Hazel jumped to her feet. "Good Lord. Go. Please," she commanded.

Hazel dashed into the hall. She followed the sounds of commotion to the opposite end of the floor and entered a bedroom where several people had gathered including Mick and Mrs. Jones.

Mr. Winthrop lay sprawled on the bed. His eyes bulged from their sockets as though he, too, was stunned.

Their young maid with sleek blond hair sat on the floor near his bed, her nakedness only partially covered by an ivory throw. She'd buried her face against the mattress, but Hazel could see from her shaking shoulders that she sobbed.

Hazel's heart lurched in sickening thumps, and she glanced at the stoic faces around her. *"Why is no one doing anything?"* She stepped forward.

Mick gripped her arm, stopping her. He shook his head. "It's too late. He's dead."

Hazel jerked her arm free. "How do you know? If it's a heart attack, maybe he can be revived."

Rachel sobbed harder. "I wanted to help." Her words came out between frantic breaths. "But he was frothing at the mouth and convulsing..." She stilled, her dark eyes wet and rimmed with red. "Like a rabid dog," she whispered.

Hazel did take a step back then. She couldn't imagine what kind of disease or disorder would make a person froth at the mouth, but it couldn't be good.

"What is it?" A feeble voice came from behind them. "What's happened?"

Hazel cringed. Mrs. Winthrop. She couldn't see this. Not her dead husband that she'd wanted to impress only moments before. Not the naked woman who'd obviously been with him doing things they shouldn't when he'd died.

No wife should ever witness something like this.

Hazel turned from the gathered crowd and met Florence in the hall. She took the woman's chilly hands in hers. "I'm so sorry, Florence." She would hide it all from her if she could. "It's your husband."

"Albert?" She shot a frantic gaze beyond Hazel's shoulder. "What's wrong?"

Hazel closed her eyes for a long moment, not wanting to be the one to deliver the news. Then she met the new widow's gaze. "He's dead."

Florence screamed and collapsed against Hazel.

"Help, please," Hazel cried out.

Mick emerged into the hall and gathered Florence into his arms. "Let's get her to bed, and you can stay with her while I call the police."

CHAPTER TWO

Hazel drew a strand of hair across her lips as she stared at Florence's slack features and pale skin. The poor woman lay on her bed, passed out from shock, and Hazel couldn't help but worry. The EMTs who'd come for Mr. Winthrop had checked her stats, said they were fine, and offered to transport her to the hospital if they were still worried. Hazel and Mick had decided to call her doctor instead.

Mick had left moments ago to make the call, and Hazel sensed she'd likely be fine. At least, physically.

The poor woman had experienced quite a shock, so maybe it was better that she was asleep. What a horrible, horrible morning, and her friend had many long, difficult days ahead of her.

Hazel gently took her hand and gave it a soft squeeze.

Florence drew in a deep breath that startled Hazel, and her eyes flew open. She stared at Hazel for a long moment as though confused, and then her face crumpled into a mask of pain. "Tell me it was a dream. Please. Tell me it's not true," she whispered.

Agony emanated from the older woman, and Hazel's heart wept along with her. "I'm so sorry, Florence."

She shook her head vehemently as though rejecting Hazel's apology. "How could this have happened? He was perfectly fine this morning, in one of his jovial moods."

Hazel squeezed her hand again. "They think he had a heart attack."

"Heart attack?" she whispered and then nodded. "I told him to slow down. That he'd end up dead. A man his age shouldn't do half the things he did."

Hazel tilted her head, wondering if she should bring up Rachel's presence in his room when he'd died, wondered if Florence knew about his indiscretions. "How do you mean?" she asked instead.

"Drinking. Smoking that cigar. Driving like a maniac. The man was seventy-four years old. He should have acted like it."

Florence's ire dissolved into a puddle of tears. "He can't really be gone. I need him, Hazel. I need him here with me. How will I go on without him?"

Heart-wrenching grief poured from the woman, and Hazel fought to remember the skills her mother had taught her to help others rid themselves of negative emotions without her absorbing the same.

Not as easy as it sounded.

She gave the woman's hand another squeeze and stood to escape the overwhelming emotions. Guilt jumped like a boogeyman from the shadows, but she refused to allow it into her space.

Hazel grabbed several tissues from the container on the antique table near her bed and handed them to Florence. "Mick is calling your doctor to ask him to prescribe a sedative and to stop by if he thinks it's necessary."

Florence nodded and released another sob.

Despair tore at Hazel. She needed to help the woman, but how?

From the corner of her eye, she spied the tea service at the table where they'd sat not long ago, before the world had crashed down upon them.

Tea. In her world, that fixed everything. Especially if it was the *right* tea.

Her mother's warning jumped in her mind like a glaring red flag. *Don't give them a reason to hurt you.*

Hazel shook it off. No one in Stonebridge would hurt her. First, none of them would ever know she'd added a little something to Florence's tea, and—

Another wail left her cringing. She couldn't let the poor woman suffer.

With her back to the bed, she dumped Florence's cold tea into her own cup and refilled the now-empty teacup with fresh hot water. She pulled her personal blend of chamomile tea that had been helping many of the ladies in Stonebridge sleep better, and, with a few whispered words, she added a little extra magic to quicken the effect and help it last longer.

She stirred with a spoon and took the cup to Florence's bedside. "Here, dear. Drink some of this. My own personal blend guaranteed to help calm your nerves."

Gratitude floated in the woman's tear-stained eyes, and she took the teacup with shaking hands. "Thank God you're here, Hazel. You really are the kindest person." A stuffy nose distorted most of her words, but Hazel still understood.

"I'm glad I was here, too. Don't worry. You won't have to endure this alone."

Tears started again, but Hazel shook her head. "Drink."

Florence did. Several sips. And then several more.

Her breaths grew more even, and the twisted tension in her face eased. "It's very good."

"Thank you." She smiled. A touch of magic helped so many things. "I'll bring more when I visit again."

Florence's eyelids drooped, and Hazel rushed forward to reclaim the cup before it tipped. "Here, let me sit this on your table. Close by in case you want more."

"Yes." She nodded and blinked several long, slow times. "I'm feeling very tired now."

"That's good." Hazel took her hand again and was relieved the anguish in her soul had dropped several levels. "Sleep is the best thing for you right now. You've had quite a—"

Florence's loud snore cut off her last word.

"Okay, then," Hazel said and smiled. "Sleep tight," she whispered as she backed away from the bed.

That concoction should keep her out for a couple of hours. By then the doctor might have prescribed sedatives.

They wouldn't work as well as her tea, but that's the way the world wanted it. At least the little town of Stonebridge did.

Hazel gathered her bag and zipped the internal compartment closed before she slung it over her shoulder. She sent off a quick text to her assistant, telling Gretta she'd been delayed and that she'd explain everything when she made it to the shop.

With that, she quietly slipped out of Florence's bedroom and closed the door.

As she turned, a man in a black jacket appeared directly before her. She slapped a hand over her mouth to muffle her cry of surprise.

CHAPTER THREE

Hazel found herself face-to-face with one of the town's police officers, Officer Parrish if his name badge was correct.

She dropped her hand from her mouth to her throat. "Oh, Blessed Mother, you scared me." She exhaled a deep breath that ended on an embarrassed chuckle. She'd noticed the handsome and impressive man with dark, wavy hair in town before but had never met him.

"Blessed Mother?" Devastatingly green eyes sparked with interest.

She inhaled, realizing the blunder of using a phrase common among witches and not so-common among the witch-fearing citizens of Stonebridge. She forced another laugh and waved away his concern. "A silly phrase my college roommate used all the time, and it stuck with me."

He arched a serious brow, bringing her attention to the long lashes framing his beautiful eyes. "Was she a witch?"

"Of course not." She did her best to keep her words lighthearted. "Do folks here really believe in such things? I thought it was an act, for tourism's sake."

Her attempts to lighten the mood had no outwardly effect on him. "People believe what they believe. Miss Hardy, I presume?"

She furrowed her brows, more than a little unnerved that he knew her name. "How did you know?"

"Small town." He lifted one side of his mouth into a smile. She swore if her mother hadn't raised her better, she would have melted right there in front of him.

"Of course. Yes. I'm Hazel Hardy. Proprietor of Hazel's Teas and Temptations."

"Temptations?"

Electricity sparked between them and then jolted straight into her ever-loving heart, leaving her bewildered. No man, especially a non-magical one had ever had that effect on her before.

"Cookies. Brownies," she managed. "Those kinds of temptations. Soon, anyway. I haven't added them to my stock yet."

He nodded in appreciation. "I see. Well, Miss Hardy, you've made an impression on the town."

Good or bad? She'd like to think good, but she'd never been an outlaw before, so this could go either way. "I have?"

"My assistant can't work without a cup of your tea on her desk. She swears by it. I suppose I should stop in one day to see what I've been missing. I like to keep my finger on the pulse of the town anyway."

"Oh. Of course. You can have a temptation tasting on the house," she said with enthusiasm. Unfortunately, her unintended flirtation flooded her face with heat. She took a small step back to limit his effect on her.

Her embarrassment seemed to draw a bigger smile from him, and then he cleared his throat. "Back to the reason I'm here, Miss Hardy."

The use of her formal name always seemed so impersonal. "Hazel, please."

He nodded, but his gaze had taken on a serious quality that left her uneasy. "Let me start by giving you a word of warning, Hazel."

His words drained all warmth and happiness from her.

"The good townsfolk of Stonebridge won't appreciate phrases such as Blessed Mother, so I'd avoid using it. Our town hasn't had a known witch live here in over seventy years, but they are as skittish as ever when it comes to the subject, so if you could find a way to forget that phrase, it will be in your best interest."

She twisted her fingers together. "Yes, sir."

His expression softened. "I'm not trying to scare you. Just, as a newcomer, you might find it helpful information."

Her posture remained stiff and alert. "Of course. Thank you."

He inched closer to her. She wanted to back away but felt she needed to hold her ground. "With that out of the way, I need to address the unfortunate incident that happened here today."

"Mr. Winthrop?"

He gave her a curt nod. "Mrs. Winthrop doing okay?"

Ice chilled her veins as she thought of the potion she'd given her, not to mention other incriminating ingredients she carried in her purse right now. She swallowed. "She's sleeping. I think the shock was too much for her."

"Probably for the best. Would you mind following me into another room for a few minutes to answer a couple of questions?"

"Of course not." In that respect, she had nothing to hide.

He rapped on the door of the bedroom across the hall. When no one answered, he turned the knob and stepped in.

Though it was sunny outside, this room sat on the shady side of the house, leaving the room shrouded with a cozy dimness. He held out a hand, palm forward, inviting her to join him.

An awkward rush of attraction coursed through her as he closed the door. She glanced around, but there was nowhere to sit except the bed. She faced him instead and folded her arms across her chest.

"Miss Hardy." He paused. "Is it Mrs. or Miss?"

She wasn't sure if she wanted him to know she wasn't married. "It's Hazel, remember?"

The corners of his eyes crinkled as he smiled. "Right. Okay, Hazel, other witnesses place you here at the time of Mr. Winthrop's death. Is that correct?"

"Yes." She widened her eyes into innocent ovals. She wasn't guilty, but his earlier reminder of the town's hatred for witches left her on guard. "I came as I have for the past four Mondays to bring Florence her tea."

"Florence? Not Mrs. Winthrop?"

Her cheeks flushed. "We've become friends. She asked me to call her Florence."

He nodded. "Like you asked me to call you Hazel."

Er...not exactly. "I suppose."

"But you're not friends with Mr. Winthrop?"

At her confused look, he continued. "You called him by his formal name instead of his first, like you did with his wife."

"No. We're not friends. Today was the first day I've seen him at the house."

He jotted something in a notebook small enough to fit in his hand. "So, you brought Mrs. Winthrop tea as you do every Monday. Did Mr. Winthrop have any?"

She frowned. "No, why would he?"

He continued to scribble. "Just dotting the t's and crossing the i's."

"Isn't it crossing the t's and dotting the i's?"

He winked, and she flushed again.

Was he flirting with her? If so, didn't he know that expression was about as lame as they came?

She cleared her throat and worked to slow her pulse. "Florence and I were the only ones to drink my tea."

She paused and widened her eyes as a thought occurred. "What difference does it make if he drank any tea unless you think it somehow caused his heart attack?"

Her thoughts kicked into high gear. "Unless it *wasn't* a heart attack."

Blessed Mother. What was he accusing her of?

The officer glanced up and caught her gaze. "I'm not at liberty to discuss the case, but at this moment, it doesn't appear he was the victim of foul play."

His statement didn't bring her any relief. "Then why all the questions? I feel like I'm on trial."

He smiled, and she wanted to punch him for causing her stress. If he wasn't so attractive...and an officer, she added for good measure, she might very well do that.

Or hex him. That would serve him right.

"Just dotting—"

"Never mind." She held up a hand. "I believe we've been over that. Do you have any more questions for me?"

He stared at her for a long moment, long enough to send a shiver of attraction racing through her. "No, that should do it. Whenever there is an unexpected death, our office does a thorough investigation."

She nodded and stood. She could appreciate that.

She made it to the closed door before another thought entered her mind, and she turned to ask him. "Wait—"

Her surprised intake of air echoed through the room. He was only inches behind her. Close enough she could smell the intriguing aftershave he wore, and she longed to lean closer and get a better sniff. Whatever it was might work very well in the new love potion, make that designer fragrance, she'd recently been experimenting with.

He reached past her and gripped the doorknob but didn't open the door. The man's nearness alone was enough to scramble her thoughts and make her confess to things she hadn't done.

After a deep breath, she collected enough of herself to be coherent.

She narrowed her gaze. "Did you bring me to an isolated room just to ask me about tea?" That seemed rather odd.

His face lit up with a smile so sexy it would light her heart for days. "That's just it, Miss Hardy."

"Hazel," she interrupted, her voice barely above a whisper.

"Before we came in here, I had no idea what you might say that might need to be kept confidential, did I? We could have discussed tea...or something else."

She blinked several times, trying to clear her thoughts. Then she focused her gaze away and looked pointedly at the doorknob. If he didn't release her soon, she'd likely spontaneously combust, something no one in her mother's coven had ever been able to perfect.

But he did, and she hurried away from him, down the hall, pretending he didn't watch her.

"Blessed Mother," she whispered under her breath when she reached the staircase. Today had been far more exciting than she'd ever expected, and it wasn't even noon yet.

"Miss Hardy?" the officer's sultry voice caught her from behind.

She paused and looked over her shoulder with a questioning gaze.

"I'll see you later, then."

She lifted her brows in a panic. "Later?"

"When I stop by to taste your temptations?"

A surprise cough bubbled up and choked her. "Yes. Stop by anytime."

She forced a friendly smile, and then did her very best not to run the rest of the way out of the house.

As she pedaled away, she wondered if he watched. The burning sensation inside her told her he did, but it could be heartburn, too. The morning had been crazy enough to sprout any number of maladies inside her, attraction to a good-looking, flirtatious, witch-fearing officer being the least.

Or the most.

She couldn't decide.

She might need some of her special chamomile tea herself.

CHAPTER FOUR

The rest of Hazel's deliveries seemed to take forever, but luckily, news of Mr. Winthrop's untimely passing hadn't hit the gossip mill just yet, relieving her of retelling the story numerous times. By the time she made her rounds to other customers on Thursday, everyone in Stonebridge would know what had happened.

In fact, the story would receive several rounds of edits and embellishments by then, so no one would need her version.

She parked her bicycle on the cobblestone sidewalk alongside the renovated, eighteenth-century brick building that now housed her teashop along with a women's clothing store and a hair salon. She couldn't have picked a better location.

Luckily, the people who'd originally been interested in the lease changed their minds at the last minute, leaving it available to her.

Good karma, she liked to think.

She dragged her weary body inside and was instantly comforted by the smell of lavender and citrus, remnants of the teas she'd crafted the day before. She inhaled and allowed the scents to infuse her body and relax her.

There might have been the tiniest bit of magic in the air as well, nothing detectable by others, but perhaps a little something she'd added to the atmosphere to make it a more enjoyable experience for her customers.

Yes, she'd promised her mother, but despite the location, the citizens of Stonebridge weren't the most trusting and had needed convincing that she owned a respectable, lovely business and her wares would enhance their lives. Which was true. She wasn't trying to pull the wool over their eyes and offer them an illusion.

But sometimes the best of intentions needed a little support, a little boost, she liked to think. And if people left her shop a little happier than when they'd entered, well, didn't that make the world a better place?

More good karma and all that.

A squeal came from the entrance to the backroom, and Gretta rushed toward her. "What...on earth...happened?" It was as though she could barely get the words out.

Two older ladies paused and looked in their direction.

Hazel discreetly pinched Gretta's arm as she smiled at the two customers. "Hello, Mrs. Lemon and Mrs. Tillens. Can I help you find anything?" she called across the store.

Smiles broke on both of their faces, and they waved back. "We're fine. Thanks, dear," Mrs. Tillens called.

Hazel gave them a friendly nod and strolled casually to the register. Gretta was right behind her. The women watched her for a few seconds, but when it seemed there would be no more excitement, they turned back to their shopping.

"Don't do anything to draw attention," Hazel said under her breath. "I don't want the teashop to become the source of rumors in Stonebridge."

Gretta widened her eyes. "I need to know what happened."

Hazel knelt and pretended to fetch something from below the counter but glanced up at Gretta instead. "Do you know Officer Parrish?"

Gretta's lips curved into a dreamy smile. "You mean Chief Peter Parrish?"

Peter Parrish. She frowned. "He's the police chief?" She'd managed to attract the attention of the town's top lawman?

Her friend fanned herself. "He's pretty hot, don't you think? But cold as December. His wife died in a terrible accident several years ago. The ladies of the town gave him a good year before they swooped in like vultures."

Gretta cringed. "I shouldn't refer to it that way since technically I was one of them, but he wants nothing to do with the feminine sort. Not even the prettiest girl in town could snag his attention."

And Hazel had thought he'd been interested in her.

Her knees wobbled so she let her bottom drop to the floor and leaned against the counter. "Really? That's better news than I could have hoped for." That meant if he did bother to stop in at her shop, it was because he was interested in tea, not her.

She exhaled and ignored the odd ache growing in her chest. She must have been so distraught by what had happened to Mr. Winthrop, or so enthralled by the chief's handsome face that she'd somehow magnified each look he'd given her, each question and statement he'd made.

Blessed Mother, she was an idiot.

Gretta stared at her with a confused look. "So, I take it, the whisperings about someone dying at the Winthrop household aren't true?"

She refocused on her friend. "No, they're true. Mr. Winthrop keeled over from a heart attack, and...we found him with their maid. Naked," she said, whispering the last word.

Two loud female gasps from the opposite side of the counter warned her of her faux pas. Slowly, she rose and faced her customers.

"Dead?" Mrs. Tillens asked. Shock and excitement swirled in her eyes.

"Whilst he was...you know?" Mrs. Lemon chimed in.

Before Hazel could answer, Mrs. Tillens leaned closer and whispered. "With another woman? A younger woman?"

They both gasped again. "The scandal," Mrs. Tillens added.

"Please." Hazel put a hand over her mouth momentarily, wishing she'd done that from the start. "I don't think you heard me right. That's not exactly what happ—"

"Of course not, dear." Mrs. Lemon waved away her concern.

"We won't say a word," Mrs. Tillens added before slipping a sly smile to her friend.

The moment the women walked out of the shop, Gretta turned to her. "They're going to tell everyone."

Hazel buried her face in her hands as shame tossed a shadow over her. "I know. I know." She hadn't meant to betray her friend. If she had some way to retract her words...

Or at least a way that didn't involve magic.

She sighed and looked at Gretta. "I need some chamomile tea."

The good kind.

CHAPTER FIVE

Warm sunshine poured through the windows in the backroom of Hazel's shop where she crafted her designer teas. The brightness of the day worked to dispel the remainder of the sadness she'd absorbed from Florence Winthrop yesterday.

Hazel had taken as much of Florence's woe that she could to help the poor woman through such a trying time, and it had left her in a low state, unable to sleep most of the night.

Well, that and the fact that she'd been a major contributor to Stonebridge's rumor mill.

Another queasy wave of unease rolled through her at the reminder. Her intent was to spread positivity and goodness in this town. Not...

She shuddered. What was done was done.

Hazel scooped dried chamomile flowers from a large container and muttered under her breath as she slowly poured them into a small tin.

"Blessed Mother, I ask of thee, grant the power of peace to this tea. Strength and resilience will be needed as well. I ask—"

"What are you doing?" Gretta's voice sent a jolt of surprise ripping through her.

Hazel squealed and swung around, unintentionally flinging the remainder of the dried flowers across the workshop like fairy dust. An apple-like scent filled the air.

Hazel put a shaky hand to her chest. "You scared the living daylights out of me."

Her assistant snickered and cast a glance at the mess Hazel had made. "Sorry," she said with a light laugh. "I didn't realize you were so jumpy, or I would have made more noise coming in."

"No, no. It's all right. I was just saying a little prayer for Mrs. Winthrop while I made her tea. I guess I was focused on that." She tried to shake off the adrenaline dump.

Spells, at least her spells, were much like a prayer. Of sorts.

"Since I'm the one who caused you to make the mess, I'll get the broom and dustpan while you finish," Gretta offered and smiled.

"Thank you. I need to get this finished and over to Mrs. Winthrop as soon as possible."

Gretta drew her brows together. "You're going back again today?"

Hazel shrugged. "She asked me to bring something to soothe her frayed nerves. Plus, she's one of my best customers. I can't exactly say no."

"True," Gretta agreed. "I guess this means she's not angry with you for spreading rumors."

Hazel clutched at her stomach. "Don't remind me."

Gretta put a hand on her shoulder and gave her a kind smile. "You're a good person, Hazel."

A rush of warmth flowed through her, strengthening the ties of friendship. "Thank you." If Hazel were ever to tell anyone about being a witch, it would be Gretta.

Hazel added a touch of lavender to the tea while Gretta cleaned, and when her assistant returned to the front of the shop to open for the day, Hazel quickly finished her spell. With a satisfied nod, she placed the lid on the tin.

"I'll be back soon," she called to Gretta. She grabbed a warm sweater because the morning was still cool and headed out the back door to where she'd parked her bicycle.

As she zoomed down tree-lined streets and past old churches, she couldn't help but compare this ride to the one she'd taken yesterday. Life had been a breezy spring day filled with nothing to worry about other than making her deliveries on time.

Then she'd come across the curmudgeonly Mr. Winthrop and all the negativity pouring off him. She'd wished she'd never have to see him again, and now she wouldn't.

Her wish had come at quite a cost to Mrs. Winthrop. Not that she considered it her fault. She didn't have that kind of power.

She turned on the road to the Winthrop house and a moment later cruised up the driveway. No one to run her down this time.

A white sedan sat where Mr. Winthrop had parked his Mercedes the day before. Nothing on the car stood out marking it as a police vehicle, but she'd lived long enough in the city to recognize an undercover unit.

Chief Parrish, perhaps?

A swift bolt of excitement coursed through her at the prospect of seeing him again. She put that out as quick as a boot stomping on a spark in the middle of a dry forest. Chief Parrish was danger with a capital D. She'd be best to remember that.

She left her bike near the side of the house as usual and made her way around back to the kitchen door. She stepped inside, and a whole host of powerful sensations slammed into her. Pain. Anger. Fear. So many feelings, which was understandable.

The kitchen was completely quiet. No sign of Mrs. Jones. No heated tea service waiting for her to take upstairs.

"Hello?" she called out.

No reply.

She placed the tea canister on the counter and headed out into the main part of the house which was as quiet as the kitchen. Stairs creaked as she moved toward the second floor.

Panic threatened when she found Florence's room empty as well.

She hurried back downstairs as fast as she could without stumbling. This time, she headed deeper into the house, an area she hadn't explored in the past because she'd had no reason to do so. She'd always come to see Florence, and she'd never seemed to leave her bedroom.

Soft murmuring voices, one male and one female, greeted her as she passed the formal dining room. She continued toward the sounds and peeked inside.

Chief Parrish sat on an old-fashioned brown settee while Florence occupied a tan chair next to him. Her heart quickened in response, and she cursed it.

The tall, nicely-muscled officer seemed awkwardly out of place on the dainty couch. Florence looked ten years older than she had the day before, which brought more sadness to Hazel.

Florence's red-rimmed, swollen eyes looked up and connected with Hazel. A watery smile appeared on her face. "Hello, dear. Thank you for coming."

Chief Parrish's gaze followed, searing her as he studied her, and a startling revelation rooted deep inside her. She had not imagined the undeniable attraction that burned in his gaze now and yesterday. "Miss Hardy."

Back to the formal use of her name, it seemed. "Hi," she answered in return. "I brought the tea you requested, Mrs. Winthrop...uh, Florence, but Mrs. Jones didn't have the tea service ready."

Florence nodded in understanding. "I gave her and the rest of the staff the day off."

"You're all alone?" In such a big house? That didn't seem like a good thing. Who would cook for her? Take care of her? Make sure she had what she needed?

"Wipe that worried look off your face, Hazel. I'm capable of taking care of myself despite what everyone thinks." A hint of strength resided in her voice that Hazel hadn't noticed before which brought her hope for the woman.

"Of course." A warm blush stole over her, and she prayed her cheeks hadn't turned bright red.

"If you could manage to find your way around Mrs. Jones's kitchen and boil some water, the kind chief and I should be finished soon."

Hazel flicked her gaze to him, and he arched a brow that made his beautiful green eyes even more seductive and turned her brain to mush.

"Of course," she repeated and then turned, admonishing herself for acting like a bumbling idiot in front of him.

Hazel entered the kitchen with more than a little trepidation running rampant through her. No one touched Mrs. Jones's kitchen. She'd made that extremely clear on multiple occasions, such as every time Hazel had visited. And now she was to rifle through her cupboards looking for a teapot and cups?

She swallowed. "Bless and protect me, dear Mother," she whispered as she opened the first cupboard.

She found what she needed in short order. It was the waiting for the water to boil that took forever. All she could think about was getting back to the other room. She wanted to see the chief again, even though she didn't want to, and she itched to know what they were discussing.

Why would he return the following day if nothing was amiss?

When the shrill whistle of the teapot broke her reverie, she startled. Heaving an exasperated sigh, she filled the teapot and added it to the tray she'd already laden with cups.

She filled only one tea strainer with the chamomile tea because she didn't need to be sleepy this morning, and she'd die if the good chief drank some of her special chamomile and realized she'd worked her magic. She filled another with her favorite citrus blend.

If the chief wanted tea, he could have that kind. She'd forgo hers.

Worries hovered in her mind as she carried the tray back down the hall. In the past, witches had been tried and, if found guilty, murdered. Chief Parrish had mentioned the residents of Stonebridge still had an aversion to witches, so what did they do now if they found one within their city limits?

She turned the corner, stepped into the room and smiled. The answer to that question was something she never wanted to find out.

The handsome chief stood as she set the tea service on the table in front of the settee. She met his gaze and shivered. "You're not staying for tea?"

"Wish I could," and she had the distinct feeling he meant every word. "But duty calls."

She licked her bottom lip and quickly drew her tongue back inside when she realized she'd drawn his attention there. "Of course."

"Don't forget you promised me a taste test at your store."

She shook her head as her heart thundered faster. "No. I haven't forgotten."

"Good." He smiled, and the warmth of it filled her, chasing away any sadness she'd absorbed that day. He glanced at Florence and then back to her. "I will see you ladies later."

Florence gave him a kind smile. "Thank you, Chief."

Hazel faltered for what to say in return. Blessed be hung on her tongue, but that wouldn't do at all. "Good day," she finally managed and turned her gaze away from him so that he wouldn't see her blush.

She focused on placing strainers in the appropriate cups and poured hot water over them while she listened for him to leave. She glanced at her watch to ensure the tea steeped the right amount of time.

"He's a nice man," Florence commented when they were alone.

"Seems so. I only met him yesterday, so I don't really know."

"His wife died a few years back. Tragic hit-and-run. Devastated him."

She tilted her head as she processed the information. Gretta hadn't mentioned an unknown person had caused the accident and then fled. "That's terrible. Poor man."

And here she was talking to another person who'd lost her spouse. "How are you doing today? I know that's a dumb question because obviously awful, but is there anything I can do to help you?"

Fresh tears sprang to the older woman's eyes. "You've already done it by bringing me more tea. I've had to cut back on the supplements I take for my aching joints because my new delivery has been delayed a week, so that along with everything that has happened... It's too much. Your special tea helps tremendously. More than you know."

Well, actually, she did know, but she wouldn't admit it. "Just make sure you don't drive after drinking it because it can make you very sleepy, especially someone who's sick or suffering like you." She mentally shrugged. As good of an excuse as any for its potency.

"I won't. I'm keeping Mick on to drive me to my doctor appointments and other things, and Mrs. Jones always does the grocery shopping." She pulled a handkerchief from her bosom and blew her nose.

Hazel's mental alarm clock dinged, and she checked her watch. Right on time. "Tea should be ready." She removed the strainer and handed Florence's cup and saucer to her, hoping her spell would work wonders for the poor lady.

Hazel sipped on her own version of what she liked to call Happy Day tea. The blend of citrus, hibiscus, and lemongrass with a touch of cinnamon lifted her spirits and gave her a lovely burst of energy...without any spells.

Sometimes, nature carried its own magic.

After a good ten minutes of more tears and chatting, Florence yawned and handed her teacup to Hazel. "I'm feeling quite tired right now, my dear. Okay if we call it a day?"

"Of course." Hazel stood. "Would you like help back to your room?"

"No." She waved her away. "The joints might ache like crazy, but I can manage. Your tea helps."

"Okay, then. I'll clean up our dishes and let myself out. Make sure to call me if you need anything. I'll stop by in the next day or two to check on you, okay?" The poor widow had enough people in the house, but Hazel wasn't sure if any of them could be called friends, and Florence needed a friend to lean on right now.

"Thank you, dear. That would be lovely."

They walked out of the room together, Florence heading upstairs while Hazel made her way back into Mrs. Jones's sacred space.

CHAPTER SIX

Chief Peter Parrish parked his police unit alongside the road in front of the historic courthouse that was now the police department. A local pastor nodded in greeting as he passed him on the cobblestone sidewalk. "Morning Father," he mumbled.

Most days, he paused to notice the quaintness of his small town, something he appreciated after spending a few years away, but today, all thoughts were on one lovely Miss Hardy.

"Hazel," he said as he entered the police station, testing the sound of her name on his tongue.

"Excuse me?" The department's administrative assistant glanced his way, her blue eyes peeking over the top of black glasses.

Margaret had piled a mound of bright red hair on top of her head like women wore back in the fifties, and he fought to contain a chuckle at her latest expression of style. The woman should be in Hollywood.

"Nothing, Margaret. Just going over the details of the Winthrop case." Or at least the woman at their house who'd captured his attention. Something in her eyes. Or maybe her smile.

Margaret shook her head, threatening to topple the massive hairdo, and looked back to her computer screen. "Always talking to himself," she said under her breath.

Let it go. He fought to keep from pointing out she'd just done the same. He didn't want to start the day with a verbal scuffle with his assistant. Her persistence always beat his patience. If she didn't do a darned good job...

He stepped inside his office and then stopped, turning back to her, unable to refrain. "Kettle?" he asked, hinting that she did just as much talking to herself.

She shifted an annoyed look in his direction. "Excuse me?"

He grinned and let it drop. "Nothing."

"Then stop wasting my time," she said and went back to typing.

He'd been at his desk for less than five minutes when Margaret entered with his morning cup of coffee. "Thanks, but you know I can get my own coffee."

He did a double take. Was that a *poodle* on her skirt? Good Lord.

"You could," she offered as she set the steaming cup that smelled like heaven on his desk and turned toward the door. "But we both know you don't make the coffee right." She didn't bother to look at him or wait for a response.

Unfortunately, she was right. Just once, he wanted her to be wrong.

He sipped the dark liquid and thought back to Hazel's offer of tea. "You like that new teashop, right?" he called to Margaret who'd resumed her seat.

She turned with an exasperated look. "Hazel's Teas and Temptations? You know I do."

He nodded and waited until she started working again.

"What's your favorite kind?"

"Are we seriously having this conversation?"

He shrugged. "Yeah. I want to know."

"Okay, then," she said with sugary sweetness. "I start my day with Majestic Mint. It gives me that boost I need to deal with obnoxious people throughout the day."

Her response drew a laugh deep from within him. As much as Margaret was a pain, her sarcastic sense of humor often made his day.

"Good. I'm thinking of switching from coffee to tea. It's supposed to be healthier, and I hear Miss Hardy will deliver. I'll order a tin of Majestic Mint for you, too."

She paused for a moment, and then a smile teased the corners of her lips. "Thank you, sir. That's very kind."

Sir? He almost snorted. "You're welcome. Now, don't you have a report to finish?"

She widened her eyes in disbelief and turned her back to him with a huff.

God bless her. He smiled. She'd kept the department in order and running when his life had fallen apart. She deserved every bit as much loyalty from him as she'd given him.

He sighed and lifted the daily briefing from the state police that Margaret had placed on his desk. It was highly unlikely that any unsolved cases from other parts of the state would drift into his little town, but he liked to stay on top of things.

Twenty minutes later, the sound of a male voice in the outer area drew his attention. Dr. Ruben Stalwart stood tall and thin in front of Margaret's desk, his wave of thick, white-blond hair as shocking as always. If Albert Einstein lived in the modern era, Dr. Stalwart might be mistaken for his twin.

Peter stood as the sixty-something man entered his office, and he held out his hand. "Good to see you, Ruben."

The doctor met his handshake with a firm one of his own. "You, too, Chief." He glanced toward the outer office. "I need to speak with you. May I close the door?"

Peter shrugged. "I fully trust Margaret to keep a confidence, but if you'd be more comfortable..."

Ruben closed the door, and both men took a seat on opposite sides of the desk. The good doctor squeezed his eyes shut and then blinked rapidly as though to clear his brain. Some might find him a bit curious, but he knew medicine.

"Albert Winthrop was murdered."

His statement caught Peter off guard. "Excuse me?" he said, and then wondered if he'd channeled Margaret. "Is this a suspicion, or do you have evidence to back up your claim?"

He released a slow, weighted breath. "I have no actual evidence, yet, thanks to that idiot, Warner, for signing the death certificate while I was out of town. He stated Albert had died from natural causes because everyone speculated he'd had a heart attack. But I'm here to tell you I don't believe that is the case."

Peter steepled his fingers and leaned forward, resting his chin on the tips. "Go on."

"As Albert's regular physician, I know the state of his health better than anyone. I monitored his heart regularly. In fact, he'd been in my office a little more than three weeks ago, and his heart along with the rest of him was perfectly healthy."

"Healthy enough for sex?" Peter asked knowing the blunt question would shock the older man, but he'd wanted to check his reaction.

Ruben coughed into his hand. "Yes. In fact, I'd prescribed Viagra for him."

"Did you know he was having sex with someone other than Mrs. Winthrop?"

The doctor's cheeks pinkened. "I told him not to mess around with that young maid of his. Adulterous affairs are against the very moral fibers upon which this town was founded."

"Rachel Parker?" he asked, needing the details confirmed.

"Yes," he hissed with a fair amount of disgust. He leaned in closer. "She's a witch," he whispered.

Peter blinked in surprise and sat back in his chair. "Those are serious accusations, Ruben, even in these times. You know there are those in town who still have issues, who still believe the witches of Redemption Pond are living amongst us, mocking our ancestors."

"Oh, I know." Exasperation rolled off him. "I do not say this lightly. But, as God as my witness, Albert himself told me they tried a lovemaking ritual that was supposed to help him not need the Viagra."

Here he'd thought he'd heard it all. "Did it work?"

A huff exploded from Ruben. "How should I know?"

"Sorry. Had to ask for the record." He scrubbed his hands over his face, trying to piece together the facts. "So, you're suggesting I should order an autopsy on the grounds that Rachel Parker might be a witch?"

His face grew redder. "Fine, leave the witch part out. But a perfectly healthy man died, and I believe the cause of his death needs further investigation. The law is on my side."

"And you'd put Mrs. Winthrop through further agony to see this done?"

Ruben narrowed his focus on Peter's face. "If your wife was murdered, wouldn't you want to know that it wasn't an accident or from natural causes? Wouldn't you want to see that person pay for his or her crime?"

Blood drained from his head even as it boiled in anger. The good doctor had played his cards well and knew Peter couldn't very well deny him after that statement. "I'll contact the coroner today."

Ruben stood and held out his hand. Peter shook it even though he didn't want to. "Thank you. I think you'll find that I'm correct in my suspicions."

Peter exhaled, trying to let go of the anger that hadn't served him once since his wife had died. "For Mrs. Winthrop's sake, I hope so."

He waited until Dr. Stalwart left his office before he picked up the phone and made the call.

Then he made a second, more difficult one to Mrs. Winthrop to inform her of the situation. She'd cried like he'd expected. He hated giving her that kind of news over the phone, but he didn't have it in him to make a second trip to her house that day.

Perhaps it would be like Ruben suggested. If it was murder, Mrs. Winthrop would be willing to endure the pain to have answers.

Just like he would have done if given the choice.

He stood, suddenly needing to get out of the stifling office. "Looks like I have further investigating to do on the Winthrop death," he informed Margaret.

"Not natural causes, I take it?" All traces of teasing impudence and sarcasm were gone.

"Not according to the good Dr. Stalwart. I've ordered an autopsy, and I'll re-interview those who were at the house to see if anything suspicious arises while we wait for results. Looks like Rachel Parker is top of my list." He patted his pants pocket. "I have my phone if you need me."

But first, he planned to stop at the teashop.

CHAPTER SEVEN

Hazel straightened tins of tea on her shelves, mentally noting which were running low. Gretta was off for the afternoon, taking her grandmother for their weekly lunch date at Cora's Cafe.

The Youthful White Tea with red currants and apples and the Wellness Energy with a mixture of green and black teas and apricot seemed to be her most popular lately.

What did that tell her about the citizens of Stonebridge? That they wanted to feel younger and that they used her highest caffeinated tea for energy. Like most people, they needed to slow down and enjoy life. Doing so would do wonders for the bags beneath their eyes and their stress levels.

In the meantime, she'd do her best to help them.

Wednesdays were typically her slow days, which was why she'd given Gretta that day off, but that also made a very long day for her. She reviewed the inventory logs. Ordered more ingredients for tea from her suppliers, and then settled in at her desk in the back room. She drew a strand of hair across her lips as she thumbed through the latest catalog of teapots, teacups, and accessories for the upcoming summer tourist season.

The bell on her door tinkled, and she exhaled a breath, glad for the distraction. Perhaps it would be June Porter, who was always up for a long conversation.

She hurried to the public area of her store and lost her breath when she found one very handsome chief standing inside her doors.

He had his head turned to the side, taking his time to look over her store as though each tin of tea or colorful teapot interested him.

"Welcome to my shop, Chief Parrish." Her heart quickened as his name left her lips.

"Miss Hardy. Or would that be Mrs.?" he asked again, his engaging smile fully in place.

"Yes," she answered with a teasing tone in her voice.

He drew his brows together as he approached the counter that separated them. "Yes? I don't believe that answers my question."

She worked to keep her breathing calm. She was certain he'd asked someone in town about her marital status by now, or he wouldn't still be flirting. But if he wanted to play, she was game.

"Of course, it does. You asked if it was Miss or Mrs., and I said yes, it was one of those, which it is."

"Ah." He lifted his chin and smiled. "Playing coy."

"Playing coy?" A snort escaped her. "Does anyone actually use that phrase anymore?"

He shrugged. "We've been called a backward town, a century or so behind the times in some ways. Most around here don't seem to mind."

She straightened items on the counter and placed pens back in their holder to avoid the direct eye contact that tended to unravel her. "Did you come to try some tea?"

"I guess I did." He seemed uncertain about his decision to do so, but she knew once she had a person in her store, she could sell them for life.

"Excellent. Follow me. I know the perfect tea for you." She moved from behind the counter to the small area she'd set up for customers who wanted to enjoy tea on the spot as well.

She'd brought in stuffed, refurbished chairs covered in bright fabrics along with antique tables she'd found at a yard sale. Along one wall, she'd placed a counter-height narrow table where a teapot waited on a warmer, surrounded by teacups and strainers. Tins of her various teas sat on shelves above it.

"How can you know the perfect tea for me?" he asked, his voice sounding close enough that if she were to stop suddenly, he'd bump into her. For a moment, she considered doing that just to see.

"Have a seat," she said, indicating the closest chairs. He chose the patterned coral one, and didn't he look so cute? Of course, she wouldn't mention that to him.

She turned her attention to the selection of teas. "You're not a fruity man."

He snorted, the sound of his laugh drawing her attention. "No, not a fruity man."

He was too handsome for his own good.

"I would say something spicy, perhaps. How about..." She closed her eyes as she ran a finger over the fronts of the lined tea tins, waiting for a spark of knowing. When it came, she stopped. "This one."

She pulled the tin from the shelf and opened it. Spiced chai had always been one of her favorites. She spooned the correct amount to a tea strainer and rested it in a dark blue cup. When she poured hot water over it, the rich scent of cloves, cardamom and cinnamon filled the air.

"It smells good." The timbre of his voice sent a shiver through her.

She smiled as she set the tea on a table in front of him. "You need to let it steep for a few minutes to get the full flavor. If you take some home, I'd suggest buying a timer, too."

"I have a timer on my phone."

She shrugged. "That works if you prefer."

He glanced between the stack of clean cups and her. "Aren't you going to join me? No one likes to drink alone."

She scanned her quiet store, unable to come up with a reasonable excuse why she couldn't and failed. "Umm...okay."

"You deserve a break, too. Right?"

"It has been a quiet afternoon, so I guess it's a good time."

Hazel fixed her a cup of refreshing mint tea, something that would keep her mind alert and not let those gorgeous green eyes of his lull her into a relaxed, flirtatious state that would lead to dangerous places.

When she'd finished, she took a seat in the turquoise chair near him. She gave him a brief smile and then focused on her teacup, letting it steep. She hadn't felt this awkward around a guy since high school.

When she couldn't stand it any longer, she glanced in his direction to find him staring at her with an odd look on his face.

"What?" she asked, acutely aware of the intense energy flitting between them.

He blinked as though coming out of a trance. "What?" he echoed.

"You were staring." She rubbed the tip of her nose. "Do I have a smudge on my face or something." She *had* been cleaning the shelves.

"No. No," he said again and smiled. "You remind me of someone from my past."

"Oh." The nervous tension inside her eased. "Well, hopefully it's someone you liked."

He nodded and graced her with a warm smile. "Very much so."

Electricity between them heightened, and she swallowed. "Your tea is ready whenever you are."

He lifted interested brows and grasped the end of the strainer. "I just take this out?"

"You can put it on the edge of your saucer. I have cream and sugar, if you'd like, but you seem like a guy who likes things as they are, not all doctored up."

He tipped his head in confirmation. "For just having met, you seem to know me pretty well."

"I have a—"

She stopped just short of telling him about her empathic abilities. Her heart thundered in her chest at her near blunder, and her mind swam with every warning her mother had plied on her as Hazel had packed her bags. "It's just...I'm a lucky guesser sometimes."

He narrowed his gaze, his focus squarely on her face, and she swore beads of perspiration broke out in response. She sipped her tea. If nothing else, she could blame her response on the heat from her cup.

He tasted his as well and gave her a nod of appreciation.

"You like it?" Pleasure from his reaction increased the warmth building inside her.

"Actually, yes." He took another sip. "Something about the spices. It's much better than I expected."

"I'm really glad to hear that. I'll send you home with a sampler, so you can try it a few more times."

"How about I take a regular tin, and one of Majestic Mint for my assistant, Margaret. She's a big fan."

"Margaret is your assistant?" Why did she not know this?

Mentally, she flipped back through the conversations she'd had with the eccentric, but smart-as-nails woman. Not once had the topic of her job come up. Margaret had been much more interested in her teas and what the properties of each could do for her.

"Yep. She keeps me whipped into shape." He shook his head, but grinned.

Hazel couldn't help but match his expression. "I can see where she might do that."

"How much do you charge for delivery? The way that woman goes through coffee and tea, I might as well set up a regular delivery."

"Oh." She blinked, surprised that he'd be interested in her services. "Are you sure? Your office is only a block and a half away."

"True." He nodded and straightened in his seat. "But I'll never hear the end of it if I ask Margaret to stop for me, and I'm sort of the forgetful type."

She drew her brows together. "You don't seem like a forgetful person."

He caught her gaze and held it. "I like things easy-peasy."

Easy-peasy? She snickered inside at his quaint, old-fashioned sayings. They were ridiculous but somehow charming at the same time.

"I'd rather pay to have you stop by every week. It will give me a chance to see your smiling face. Something to look forward to."

Blessed Mother. He was flirting with her again. She wanted to ask why he'd be interested in her when he'd passed on the other town-ladies. She certainly wasn't the smartest or most beautiful.

"Um...okay," she said. "But I'd feel bad charging you for it. I pass that way when I'm headed to the Winthrop house on Monday, so it's no bother to drop it by."

"I don't mind paying."

She shook her head. "It's no problem. I'm happy to have another regular customer."

He tilted his head, and the light caught his eyes, making them sparkle. "I hope I'm more than another customer."

She choked on her tea.

"Friends?" he offered.

She cleared her throat and smiled. "Of course. Friends."

He made room for his teacup on his saucer. When he pulled a small notebook from his jacket pocket, she tensed.

He lifted a guilty gaze to her. "I have to admit, Ms. Hardy, that I've come here with dual motives. If you don't mind, I have some official questions for you."

CHAPTER EIGHT

The switch in Chief Parrish's demeanor was slight, but Hazel noticed. Fun and games were over, and this was serious. "Ms. is it now?" she asked. "Instead of Miss or Mrs.?"

As much as the flirtatious side of him made her nervous, she preferred that over this man who was all business.

He cracked a small smile, giving her a taste of relief. "Apparently. At least until you tell me which it is."

Her breath came faster. Did she dare? It might distract him from whatever serious business he was about. "It's Miss."

The smile he gave her darn near did her in. "I know."

"You know?" She drew her brows together in mock surprise. "Then why ask me?"

"Because a woman who is available and open to interested men will let that be known. One who isn't, won't."

Her jaw dropped, and she quickly closed it. How could she possibly respond to that without drawing herself in deeper?

She cleared her throat. "You said you have questions for me?"

He laughed, obviously entertained by her quick change of topic, drawing a heated blush to her cheeks. "Yes, I do." He managed to tuck away his smile as he flipped the pages on his notebook, but warm, interested feelings still reached out to her.

She mentally pushed them away.

He switched his gaze back to her. "Can you give me an accounting of your time the morning Mr. Winthrop died?"

Blood drained to her feet, and a chill descended upon her. "Why—why do you ask? I thought Mr. Winthrop died from a heart attack."

The chief released a long sigh. "That was our initial expectation, but some new information has come to light, and we will be conducting a full investigation including an autopsy. So, I ask you again, can you give me an accounting of your morning, including who you saw and spoke with?"

Murder? Hazel's insides shook as she did her best to provide the chief with an accurate accounting.

She thought about mentioning that Mr. Winthrop almost ran her over but decided against it. The incident really had no bearing on his case, and she didn't relish the idea of explaining that she'd been bucked from her bike.

He took notes while she talked and didn't interrupt to ask questions until she finished.

"Did he interact with Mrs. Winthrop at all while you were with her?"

She shook her head. "I sort of got the impression he didn't want much to do with her. I guess a younger mistress on the side would explain that."

He directed a sharp gaze at her. "You're referring to Rachel Parker?"

She gave a small shrug. "She was with him at the time he died. They were both...naked," she said, ending on a quiet note.

"You were aware of their affair?"

"No," she quickly denied. "Honestly, I've only been going to see Mrs. Winthrop once a week for a month. I always enter through the kitchen, see Mrs. Jones who has a tea service prepared for me, and I take that directly upstairs to Mrs. Winthrop."

She frowned as another memory flitted into her mind.

"What is it?" the chief demanded.

She bit her bottom lip as she peered at him from beneath lowered brows. "I hate to say anything because I just don't see how..."

"You need to tell me what you know, Hazel. Every detail. It's important."

He'd called her Hazel, and she liked it. She blew out a breath, trying to concentrate and not wanting to implicate anyone innocent. "It's really a silly thing. I'm sure it's nothing."

He arched an impatient brow.

She wouldn't get out of this. "When I arrived, Mrs. Jones was in a very good mood."

He waited expectantly.

"She's never in a good mood. Like *ever*," she explained. "She's one of the sourest people I know."

"You've seen her four times including this one. Do you feel that is sufficient to judge her character?"

Hazel threw her hands upward in frustration. "I told you it was silly. You're the one who made a big deal of it."

He held his palms outward in a show of defeat. "Nothing is silly. It's worth noting in any case."

She folded her arms across her chest, not liking this official questioning at all.

When he finished writing, he met her gaze again. He eyed her folded arms and then released the stiffness in his shoulders. "I'm sorry. The detective in me gets carried away sometimes."

"I'm not on trial then?"

"I have no reason to suspect you, Miss Hardy."

Except now he was back to Miss Hardy. The man frustrated her beyond reason.

He studied her for a long moment and then sighed. "I have one more question, and then I'll get out of your hair. Did you ever see or hear anything that might be considered witchcraft?"

A chill crept over her. "Excuse me?" she managed.

"I know it's a delicate subject that most don't wish to discuss. But a certain person gave information that Miss Parker had explored a spell with Mr. Winthrop at some point. With the history of this town and the natural aversion to witchcraft that most still carry, I have to consider it as a possible connection."

"How?" she demanded. When he'd said the fine folks of Stonebridge lived in another century, he wasn't kidding.

He tilted his head to the side as though weighing the information for himself. "Maybe he threatened to talk about their ritual, and she hexed him to keep him quiet."

He paused for a moment. "Or perhaps she created a toxic substance and poisoned him. Being labeled a witch can still carry serious consequences in this town. People won't fill the accused's pockets with stones and throw them into Redemption Pond like they did so many years ago, but..."

She drew in a sharp, shocked breath. "People really did that?"

He drew his brows together as he studied her closer. "Did you pay attention in history class?"

Sort of. She hadn't gone to regular school, and her history lessons tended to be different than others.

"I might have fallen asleep a time or two," she said sheepishly, trying to downplay her unexpected reaction. "I still can't believe they'd just kill them."

"They were witches," he said as though that was a sufficient reason.

"They were people," she countered.

"Not good ones."

She worked to keep her breaths slow, even as her heart thundered. "Are you saying all witches are bad?"

He stared at her for a long moment, and she ached to cast a forgetful spell on him, run home and pack up her stuff, and never return to Stonebridge.

Instead of pressing her further for her lack of knowledge, he pocketed his notebook and stood. "Thanks for answering my questions and for the tea. If I think of anything else, I'll be in contact."

She got to her feet, accepting his façade that everything was kosher between them when she knew it wasn't for her, and she sensed a deep rumbling of curiosity in him, too.

"Okay. If I think of anything else, I'll let you know, too."

He held out his hand, and she shook it. Panic sprouted when he kept his fingers folded around hers, with his middle and forefinger on her wrist. "If I may, I'd like to give you a few more bits of friendly advice."

She nodded, unable to trust her voice to create coherent words.

"Since you've decided to make Stonebridge your home for now, you might want to visit the local library and catch up on some history. I think you'll find it will help you to navigate the town's customs and quirks much easier."

Was that a warning? "Okay."

After a few seconds of unnerving contact, he released her, and she tucked her hand against her stomach as though she'd been burned.

He smiled. "Don't forget to deliver tea for Margaret and me. Which day did you say?"

"Monday," she managed.

"Perfect. I'll see you then. Would you mind picking out a teapot and a couple of those tea holder thingies and bring them, too? I'd be grateful."

"Of course." She exhaled and gave him a warm, if forced, smile. "I'll see you then."

He dipped his head in farewell and strolled out of her shop as though he hadn't completely tipped her world upside down.

The second he was gone, she dropped into a chair, her shaky legs no longer willing to hold her. She buried her face in her hands and took several deep breaths.

She wasn't an imbecile. She'd heard of the horrifying Salem Witch Trials and the travesties bestowed upon people of her kind, but she hadn't known that had happened here, in a town her great, great grandmother several times over had once lived.

Was that why her family had left the area so long ago, supposedly fleeing in the middle of the night?

As soon as she finished her deliveries in the morning, she'd hurry over to the library. She could steal an hour to investigate the quaint and charming Stonebridge's bloody history and how that might have intersected with her family.

CHAPTER NINE

Under the guise of marketing, Hazel headed out the next afternoon, leaving Gretta in charge of the shop for the rest of the day. It wasn't a complete lie. Hazel had brought along a few sample packs of her most popular teas. She placed them in her basket, hopped on her bike and rode the short distance to the library and parked along the side.

According to a plaque on the side of the building, the town's library was housed in a lovely historic structure built from rock that had been hauled in from a quarry back in the 1700s. The building had once been the hub of activity in Stonebridge including school, church, and social gatherings of all kinds.

She found it hard to believe something manmade could withstand the ravages of time and still look this good. The people of the town for generations had obviously taken excellent care of it. That kind of pride seemed to be missing in the bigger cities where she'd lived.

Or maybe she'd been around the wrong kinds of people. Despite its dark history, she liked this quaint town and the slower way of life. She liked getting to know the names of people she passed on the street. Liked having them know her and smile in return.

She lifted her care package from the basket on her bike and headed inside.

The scent of things timeworn tickled her nose, and she withheld the urge to sneeze. An aged wooden counter that shone with polish separated her from the overweight young man who stood behind it.

Half of his white shirt was tucked in his pants while the other side had come loose. Dark, unruly curls topped his head, and the smudged glasses he wore had slid part way down his nose.

Confidence emanated from him despite his disorganized appearance, but she detected something of a negative vibe from him.

"Hello," she said with a smile, waiting to make up her mind about him. "I'm Hazel Hardy. I've recently opened the teashop over on Main Street."

"Hi. Yeah, I've seen the place."

The teas might be wasted on him, but one never knew. Maybe his mother drank tea.

She lifted the gift package. "I stopped by to do some research and thought I'd bring some samples for you."

She glanced beyond him. "And any co-workers. The head librarian, maybe?"

"It's just me. Timothy Franklin, at your service. I am the head librarian and everything else," he said as he accepted her gift and sniffed. "Smells good."

"I hope you like them," she said hopefully.

Timothy grunted, set them aside, and then focused on her. "Is there something I can help you find?"

"Since I'm new to town, I wanted to learn more about Stonebridge's history. There are so many beautiful buildings like this one and pretty places."

He eyed her with an even gaze. "You're looking for more information on the witches."

He didn't even phrase it as a question. Apparently, she wasn't the first curious customer. "Yes." No sense in lying.

"Had you pegged the moment you walked in. Follow me." He walked from behind the counter and down an end aisle toward the back of the library.

She rolled her eyes as an embarrassed flush heated her cheeks. *He couldn't have known.* He was just guessing.

"Everything we have is in this area right here." He pointed to a small section of books on the bottom level, some of which looked as though they'd been well-used.

"Thank you." Despite what Chief Parrish had said about how the town could be unfriendly, she hadn't found that to be the case except Mr. Winthrop. And maybe Mrs. Jones.

The librarian started to walk away and then stopped. "We also have a special section we keep locked that can only be viewed at the front desk in my presence. A collection of old books and diaries, some dating back to the town's original settlement."

She widened her eyes and her pulsed kicked up a notch. "Really?" She tried to sound as interested as the average person. "I'd love to look at those, too."

He nodded, his smile smug. "Thought you might. Start here first, though. This will give you an overview of the town's history and its residents. Then the other books will have more meaning."

Disappointment rolled through her as she glanced at the section of books before her. She wouldn't get through those in a day. "Sounds like a plan."

With that, he left her. She knelt, ensured she was alone in the aisle and closed her eyes, trying to use her senses to help decide where to start.

When nothing came to her, she picked, "Stonebridge: An Accounting of the First Inhabitants".

She spent an hour reading about the town's original inhabitants including the moral and righteous John Henry Parrish. A distant relative of Peter's? Did his roots go that deep?

The book went on and on about John's wonderful works and the things he did to help the town grow into a prosperous community. He seemed like a good chap.

She flipped a few pages, read the chapter title, and lost her breath.

A Blight on the Community.

Her frown grew larger as she read about the fear and disgust of discovering miscreants among the residents of their township. Witches. Monsters of human society. Those who would confuse the minds of good people, steal their ability to worship God in all his glory.

She licked her dry lips and kept reading. The discovery of more witches. The hatred.

A copy of a written document outlining how they planned to rid their town of this blight by trying and condemning these witches. By binding their hands, filling their pockets with stones, and pushing them off a boat into the deepest water of Redemption Pond.

She paused and closed her eyes as a wave of nausea rolled through her.

They'd murdered those poor, innocent people. All because of fear of something they didn't understand. Something they didn't want to understand.

The Named.

She sucked in an audible breath and then quickly checked to ensure she was still alone.

As fast as her eyes would allow her, she scanned the list of names which included whether they'd been found guilty or innocent, and if guilty, their punishment.

Clarabelle Foster Hardy. Guilty. Death by drowning.

She clutched her stomach and tried to breathe.

This town had murdered one of her family. No wonder her mother had been so adamant that she not come here. But if she knew what had happened, why hadn't she told Hazel?

Images of women, bound and frightened, sitting in a boat as it was rowed to the deepest part of the pond slammed into her mind like a bird flying full speed into an unseen window. Fragments of fear, real or imagined threatened to bring her to her knees.

She closed the book. Tried to breathe.

Slowly, she filled her lungs, exhaled, and repeated the process several times until her emotions steadied. When she felt she could hold her demeanor, she pulled two more random books from the shelf and headed toward the front.

At the counter, the librarian glanced up expectantly. "Find what you were looking for?"

She forced a lighthearted smile. "It's all very interesting. Am I able to borrow these and read at home?"

"Sure." He pulled a form from under the counter. "Fill this out with your information, and I'll get these ready to go for you."

Hazel wrote her information and watched Timothy pull cards from the back of each book. He stamped dates on similar blue cards and replaced the original cards.

"You're not computerized?" she asked.

"Nah. The town considered it a while back, but we're a small library in a small town and function just fine the way we are."

He shrugged. "I don't mind. Sometimes I wish I was born in a different era. In some ways, things were better three hundred years ago. Simpler."

She snorted in disagreement and then covered it with a smile. "Unless you were a witch."

"Yeah," he agreed. "But the town managed to take care of that infestation and haven't had many problems since. Good, old-fashioned pest control."

She blinked, doing everything she could to keep from screaming as she gathered her books. If she didn't find fresh air soon, she'd likely combust or curse him. "Thanks for these. I'll make sure to have them back on time."

"Sounds awesome, Miss Hardy." He paused and glanced at the books in her hand. "If you read far enough, you'll learn about a witch with the last name Hardy."

Blood drained from her head and left her dizzy. She fought through the fog for an acceptable response. "Really?"

"Don't worry," he said with a chuckle. "There's another witch with my last name, too."

A relieved laugh burst from her. "Oh, good. For a moment, I was a little panicked."

"In fact, the town's most haunted house belonged to a witch named Clarabelle Hardy." He tilted his head as though waiting for her reaction.

No wonder it was haunted, with the way they'd killed her. "Here, in town? I haven't heard of a haunted house."

He grinned. "We have a few. Stick around long enough, and you'll learn more."

"Does someone live in her house? Maybe one of my customers?" she asked with lighthearted curiosity, working to keep her disdain in check in case he was sensitive to that sort of thing.

He snorted. "People move in and out. The last was over a year ago, but they got spooked and relocated after a few months."

"That's ridiculous." She snorted. "I don't believe in ghosts."

"Some in town would argue otherwise."

She shrugged, playing along. "I guess if I get the opportunity, I'll have to look for myself." It was the perfect excuse to get inside her dearly-departed one's house. If Clarabelle really was there, she'd sense her.

"Take a left on Vine until you reach Hemlock. The house is just after you cross the old bridge. You'll know it when you see it. Gorgeous First Period home. I'd love to get my hands on it and restore it to its original glory, but I doubt Clarabelle would like that."

She drew her brows together. "Why's that?"

He puffed his chest. "Direct descendant of John Henry Parrish."

The hairs on her arms stiffened. No wonder she'd gotten a negative vibe from him the moment she'd walked in even though he'd been perfectly nice. "Any relation to Chief Parrish?"

He gave her a smug smile. "Not that I can trace."

Tainted family blood could be cleansed, but only if a person was willing. Timothy obviously was not.

She'd need to be careful whenever she was in his presence. Which led her to wonder who else in town might be a threat if they knew her heritage. Perhaps, in time, they might come around.

She smiled. "I guess I know who to ask if I have questions about the town."

"Always at your service." He bowed, the act tugging more of his white shirt from his pants. "You have a good day, now. Enjoy that beautiful weather."

"Thank you. I will." She turned and strolled from the library, wishing she could take a shower and wash off the horrible feelings that covered her like sludge.

Warm sunshine radiated on her as she emerged from the old building and placed the borrowed books in her bike's basket, but she shivered.

Peter was right. Stonebridge had a dark side that wasn't noticeable at first glance but had the potential to be deadly all the same.

CHAPTER TEN

Hemlock Street. Just off Vine.

Only a few blocks from where Hazel stood in front of the library.

She glanced at her watch. It wasn't that late in the day and shouldn't take long to cruise by and get a glimpse of her ancestral home.

Decision made, she hopped on her bike and pedaled faster than normal down Main, hanging a left at Vine. With all this cycling, she'd surely drop a few of those pounds that seemed determined to remain lifelong friends.

She hoped.

She wound along Vine Street, over the picturesque stone bridge with water drifting beneath it, and continued until she reached the street sign that said Hemlock. With excitement bubbling inside, she turned onto that road and directed her gaze farther down the road, just past the bridge.

A large grove of trees nearly cloaked the white house huddled beyond them.

As she drew closer, a wave of euphoria caught her by surprise. She glanced toward the elms and birch trees and inhaled. So much beautiful, untainted energy. Like nothing she'd encountered before, and she couldn't ignore the powerful invitation. It filled her heart, as though it was calling her home.

"Blessed Mother," she whispered, awed and bewildered by the experience.

The house came into view, and she smiled. She rode until she stood before the two-story white home with pitched gables and a black roof. Round windows had been placed in both gables, and a small covered porch sat to the right of the front door.

A weathered, crooked sign announced that it was for sale and appeared to have been for a while. Time and neglect had chipped away at the exterior but still couldn't hide the beauty of the home. If she had the money, she'd make an offer on it right now.

A soft breeze picked up and whispers of welcome whistled through the trees. She closed her eyes and opened her heart to whatever was in the area.

There. That was it.

The familiar urge that had burned in her for months before she'd moved to Stonebridge emerged. She hadn't recognized it as more than curiosity about her family at the time, but this was the siren's call that had brought her here.

As for ghosts?

Oh, yes. She definitely sensed a female presence, but not the malevolent one the librarian had spoken of. This entity was warm, yet powerful. Inviting and more than a little interested in her.

She parked her bike behind a bush on the side of the house so that it wouldn't draw attention and walked to the front porch. After indulging in a quick glance around the quiet area, she tested the doorknob.

Locked.

She grumbled beneath her breath. "How am I supposed to learn more about you if I can't get inside?"

Prepared to leave, she jerked on the doorknob one more time and gasped when it turned. She'd been around witches and wiccans all her life and had seen some amazing things, but this freaked her out a little.

She took one more glance over her shoulder, stepped inside and closed the door.

Eerie sensations mixed with something familiar drew her farther inside the dust-infested home. A fine layer of soot on the once-polished wooden floor showed that no one had come inside the home for quite some time. Because they were afraid of a ghost.

Clarabelle's ghost.

"Hello?" she called.

When nothing answered, she laughed at herself. What had she expected? An apparition welcoming committee?

The sound of something crashing to the floor brought her gaze around sharply, and she cast an eye toward the ceiling. If she hadn't continued to sense that warm presence, she would have fled.

Instead, she carefully made her way to the narrow staircase. Step by creaking step, she ascended until she arrived on the second floor.

The house had a total of four rooms upstairs. She spotted the two round windows she'd seen from outside, one in each room at the front of the house, and then two more rooms, one on each side of her.

She investigated the rooms at the back of the home first, finding nothing more than a few pieces of old, broken furniture and more dust.

When she stepped into one of the rooms at the front of the house, something to the side of her moved. She screamed and whirled toward it.

A ginger-colored cat hissed in response and arched as it backed away from her.

"Oh my gosh." She brought a hand to her heart where her pulse thumped wildly, and then she gave a soft laugh.

She knelt so she wouldn't appear as threatening and held out a hand. "I'm so sorry. I scared you as much as I did myself."

The cat, a male she sensed, eyed her with quiet disdain and made no move forward.

"Really, I'm sorry," she tried again. "How did you get in here?"

The cat must be able to access the house some way because he looked a healthy weight, and she was certain there weren't enough mice in the house to sustain the feline if he'd somehow been left or locked in.

She took a cautious step toward it. The cat crouched down and then suddenly glanced to the side of him, enough of a reaction that Hazel did the same to see what he looked at, but nothing was there.

Then the ginger feline bolted from the room.

"Sorry," she called after him, feeling bad that she'd invaded his home and frightened the poor thing.

She turned to leave and then found the cat in the doorway to the bedroom watching her with intense green eyes. For a quick moment, an odd feeling passed over her but then dissipated.

"Don't worry," she said as she moved toward the doorway. "I won't be here long. I just wanted a look around."

He backed away as she slipped past.

Feeling more and more like an intruder, she took a quick peek in the remaining room, found nothing, and headed for the stairs. Disappointment washed over her.

No ghost other than a feeling. Nothing but empty rooms and an irritated cat.

She had gotten that familiar feeling upon entering, but nothing like what she'd received when passing the grove of trees next door.

She'd almost made it to the bottom of the stairs, when the ginger cat rushed between her legs, the surprise causing her to misstep. The back of her heel grazed the edge of the stair below her, and she lost her balance.

The wooden steps bit deep into her flesh as she flailed and tumbled the rest of the way down.

She landed at the bottom with a hard thud that stole her breath.

She lay there for a moment in disbelief.

Carefully, she moved each limb, testing for anything that felt like a break. When all seemed in passable condition, she moved to a sitting position.

From the corner of her eye, she caught sight of the ginger and found him sitting on the second step.

"You!" She pointed a harsh finger in his direction. "You tried to murder me."

He only stared.

After a long showdown, the cat turned his gaze toward the stairs where he sat. Then he glanced back at Hazel. When he did the same thing a second time, a tingle rippled over her.

The sensation that he wanted something overwhelmed her.

She scooted on her bottom closer to where the cat sat. When she was within striking distance, the feline dashed up the stairs.

"Yeah," she called after him. "Don't think I'm going to forget this anytime soon."

With the cat out of the way, she looked closer at the step that he'd seemed so interested in. One side sat higher than the other, and if she compared it with all the other steps, she could see where it might seem a little out of place.

She grasped the lip of the step and lifted. It didn't move easily, but it did move. With a little more effort, she opened it.

She found the hinges on the inside quite ingenious, but it was the plain wooden box sitting inside that set her heart to beating faster. She lifted it out, causing a thick layer of dust to scatter into the air. She sneezed and sent more flying.

Her fingers sizzled with excitement as she lifted the lid. Inside lay a tome that, from the looks of it, she knew Timothy would love to get his hands on. Worn brown leather with tooled symbols protected whatever was inside, and she knew darn well that people didn't hide ordinary books.

With gentle fingers, she opened the cover.

Elaborate handwriting had been scrawled over the first page. *Book of Spells. Clarabelle Foster.*

Beneath her name was a quote. *Better to follow your heart, or you're already dead.* Wow.

If she'd thought falling down the stairs had knocked the wind out of her, that was nothing compared to this.

Her hands shook as she carefully turned a few pages. How could it have remained hidden all these hundreds of years? Had her family been afraid to remove it after the town had drowned Clarabelle? What had happened to Clarabelle's husband?

Obviously, she'd been married and had at least one child, or Hazel wouldn't be alive.

"*Meow.*"

She lifted her gaze to find the mischievous feline only a few steps above her. "This doesn't forgive what you did." She had no doubt of the reason behind the cat's antics now, but that didn't mean her whole body didn't hurt like the dickens.

"*Meow,*" he said louder, his tone seeming more urgent.

"What? I've found what you wanted me to and now you want me to—"

Go! Now!

An ethereal voice echoed through the house or through her head. She didn't know. But it was adamant that she leave immediately.

She didn't question. Her mother taught her better than to doubt her senses. She winced as she climbed to her feet.

With shaking hands, she tucked the tome beneath her shirt and into the waistband of her jeans. Her ankle screamed in protest as she hurried toward the front door, but she couldn't slow.

A quick peek out the window assured her no one was close by, and she slipped outside, closing the door behind her. She didn't slow to check to see if it locked.

She strode to her bike, ignoring the pain of each step. Blocked by the bushes, she removed the tome and tucked it amongst the other books in her basket. She slipped a leg over her bike and pushed off.

Her first attempt at pedaling speared her ankle with a searing pain that culminated with her trying to stop the bike, only to crash to the ground once again, this time scraping her palms over rough gravel and dumping the contents of her basket.

The sound of an engine brought panic. She crawled and gathered the books, stuffing them into the basket as she hobbled to her feet. She didn't look up as the vehicle approached, and she did her best to look as inconspicuous as possible as she pushed her bike away from the house.

The vehicle slowed, and she cursed.

When it was next to her, she glanced over.

Of course. With her luck, it would be none other than the gorgeous yet likely dangerous Chief Peter Parrish.

He lowered his window and nodded at her bike. "You okay?"

"Yeah. I'm good."

"Then why are you limping? And if I'm not mistaken, you have blood on your hands."

She glanced down and found several spots where the gravel had torn into her flesh, leaving crimson evidence in its wake. She momentarily closed her eyes and sighed. "I took a little tumble, but I'm fine."

"You don't look fine." He put his cruiser in park and opened the door, drawing panic deeper into her heart. She didn't dare glance at Clarabelle's spell book for fear of drawing his attention, but he was far too close for comfort.

"Really. I'm fine." She waved him away with a flick of her hand. "You can be on your way."

He caught her hand and turned it palm upward. Traitorous beads of blood glistened. He held it while he looked over the rest of her. "If you were fine, you would have been on your bike riding. Instead, you're hobbling like..."

He released her hand and knelt in front of her. Warm fingers encircled her damaged ankle, and he squeezed.

Her gasp came involuntarily.

He stood. "Just as I thought. Looks like you could use a ride home. With your ankle swollen like that, you shouldn't be walking or riding."

She shrugged and shook her head in denial. "I can't leave my bike." As though that was a perfectly good reason to stay.

He leaned closer until his nose was only a few inches from hers. "It *will* fit in my car, you know. Grab your books and get in."

"If I don't?"

He narrowed his gaze and snorted. "Are you always this stubborn?"

"Are you?" she countered.

A long moment drew out as he studied her eyes, leaving her heated and uncomfortable. "Yes," he finally said. He reached for the books.

"*Wait.*"

He paused and turned to her.

She intercepted the books, clutching them against her. "I'll go willingly, officer."

Her compliance brought an engaging grin to his face. "Smart lady."

He leaned her bike against the car while he helped her into the passenger seat. "Looks like you took me up on my suggestion," he said and tipped his head toward the books.

She gave a quick nod before she faced forward, and he closed the door.

It took him a moment to wrangle her bicycle into his trunk, and she decided it served him right for being so insistent. Though she was ever so grateful to be off her foot. Even now, she could feel the blood pooling as it swelled bigger.

She'd ice it tonight, and then a long soak in Epson salts and ginger root would do her a world of good.

As soon as he climbed into the car, a frisson of energy swirled between them again.

She had to somehow put a stop to it before their flirtations went any further, but she wasn't sure how. She could tell him what she was and cool the attraction instantly, but she'd also put herself in jeopardy. She'd have to leave Stonebridge immediately if he didn't arrest her on site, and she wasn't ready to do that just yet.

She held the books close to her chest. She'd just found something very valuable to her and wanted to learn much, much more about her family's history that intertwined with the town's.

"I have a question," she said tentatively.

"What's that?" He glanced out the back window and pulled out onto Hemlock.

"Rachel...Parker. What will happen to her if she is a witch? That's not really a crime around here these days, is it?"

He released something that resembled a chuckle, but it held no humor. "It's not an official crime. Nothing she can be punished for in traditional courts."

He flicked a quick sideways glance at her. "You've heard of the KKK?"

She nodded.

"Stonebridge has its own version of that regarding those involved in witchcraft. People have been known to disappear. To die mysteriously. She'll need to be careful until we get this figured out."

Hazel widened her eyes in fear. "Does she know that?"

If Rachel had been an actual witch, she might not have feared as much for her. During the past three hundred years, since those terrible times, witches had grown stronger and practiced more in the art of self-defense. Not that they weren't still vulnerable if caught, but the playing field was more even.

"She's being careful. I questioned her this morning, and of course, she denied being a true witch. She's staying with her brother on Beck Street, and he knows how to use a gun. If she doesn't go anywhere alone or go out at night, she should be safe enough."

She shook her head, trying to form a coherent thought. "I'm shocked. Stonebridge seemed like such a friendly place when I arrived. Outsiders would never guess such things take place here."

"Luckily, we don't have many incidents. The smart people involved in witchcraft left centuries ago. The less than smart, well, they're no longer around, either."

A terrifying shiver enveloped her. What did that make her then?

"Thank you for the ride," Hazel said when he pulled in front of the small house she'd rented not far from her shop. She opened her door. He was out of the car and around to hers before she'd managed to get on her feet.

Problem was, the foot she needed to put weight on to emerge was also her damaged ankle.

"Cross your arms in front of your books and give me your elbows," he suggested.

She did as he asked, and his warm fingers cupped her skin, giving her shivers as he hauled her to her feet. Standing only inches from him, she glanced up. A quick energy-charged moment passed and then he stepped back.

"If you like, I can carry you into your house."

"No." Oh, no. That was not happening. "I can make it just fine. But thank you again for the ride. If you wouldn't mind putting my bike between my car and the house, I would be so grateful."

He tilted his head. "Anything for the lady."

She gave him a warm smile and headed for her door. Her fingers shook as she unlocked it and stepped inside. She couldn't resist a quick glance back before she closed it.

He hadn't moved. He'd been waiting to ensure she made it fine before he handled her bike.

Blessed Mother help her.

Why couldn't she have found a guy like him in the city? One who didn't despise the blood that ran red in her veins?

She waved goodnight and closed the door.

After he drove away, she grabbed an ice pack from the freezer, climbed into bed and propped up her foot. Then she opened her grandmother's book. Fierce energy bolted through her, and she gasped at the intensity.

She flipped through several pages, the energy growing stronger with each turn until nausea rose inside her and inhaling became a chore. She'd heard of lost books and buried objects becoming saturated with magic to the point they could turn lethal, and she quickly closed the tome.

She'd give it some time in the moonlight to cleanse and settle things before she opened it again. Just in case.

CHAPTER ELEVEN

When Hazel made her deliveries the next day, she drove instead of biking, with her ankle wrapped tightly. It was unfortunate, but if she wanted a quick recovery, she'd have to take it easy for a few days longer. Her magic baths, as she liked to call them, helped tremendously, but her body still needed time to heal.

Gretta had offered to take over the delivery duties, but Hazel couldn't stand the thought of being cooped up all day, not after the infusion of energy she'd received yesterday from the special grove of trees and finding Clarabelle's book of spells. The strength encased in that book had left her skittish.

And then there was her interaction with Peter.

She wished he didn't affect her like he did, but that was a consequence she'd have to deal with during her stay in Stonebridge.

The bright side of driving was that she finished her regular rounds in record time, which left her time to stop by to visit Mrs. Winthrop and one other person before her.

Hazel had bypassed second thoughts and gone on to thirds by the time she parked in front of the small home where she'd discovered Rachel Parker had taken up residence since leaving the Winthrop household.

She hoped visiting Rachel wouldn't be a huge mistake for her or Rachel, but she had questions and needed answers. It would be bad enough for Rachel to be convicted, whether in a court or otherwise for a crime she didn't commit, but she didn't want any more blood to be shed in the name of silencing witches.

She opened the weathered white picket gate and proceeded a few steps up the walk and then stumbled to a halt. Her eyes grew wide in horror.

On the white front door where Rachel stayed, someone had spray painted witch in blood red along with a haphazard inverted pentagram, marking the house and its inhabitants.

"Blessed Mother, protect them," she whispered.

She swallowed the bile in her throat and continued toward the door. Hatred flew off it in waves.

The hatred of uneducated people.

She lifted a hand and knocked, working to keep the angry feelings from penetrating her psyche.

Hazel had packaged up a few of her soothing teas to leave as a gift, and she hoped that they, along with a friendly face, would give her admittance into Rachel's private world.

A gruff looking man with unkempt blond hair and a long goatee answered the door. "What do you want?"

Rachel's brother, she assumed. Hazel opened her heart and gave him her kindest smile. "I'm here to see Rachel, if she's up to visitors. We only met once at the Winthrop house, but I'm worried about her welfare. With this town the way it is, I don't expect that she's received much support, and I'd like to give her mine." She sent him a hopeful glance.

He stepped back to let her enter. "You could have stopped at I'm here to see Rachel. She's in the kitchen." He jerked his head toward the back of the house and fell into a worn recliner where it seemed he spent a fair amount of time by the looks of it.

Scents of rotting food or old garbage assaulted Hazel as she closed the front door behind her. She didn't fail to notice the handgun on the table next to the chair as she made her way toward the kitchen.

Peter had been right. He apparently could protect her as long as she didn't leave the house.

Hazel found Rachel sitting at a table cluttered with dirty dishes. A shell of the vibrant woman she'd met the first time she'd delivered to the Winthrop household stared out a large picture window into a tree-filled backyard. She'd knotted her blond hair on the top of her head in a messy bun, and the once-slender woman now looked ghastly thin.

"Hello, Rachel," Hazel said as she entered.

Rachel turned dull eyes in her direction, but then a hint of a smile crossed her lips. "Hazel, right?"

"Yes." She strode to the table and took a seat next to Rachel. "Beautiful fall leaves. The colors seem much brighter here than in the city."

She nodded, but the dismal expression on her face hinted that she didn't care much for what the season brought, and who could blame her.

"I brought you some tea. A peach blend to soothe your nerves, and my special chamomile tea in case the stress is keeping you from your sleep."

She snorted. "You've summed up my life pretty well, Hazel."

The sadness and fear emanating from the young woman tugged at Hazel's heart. "I'm so sorry. You don't deserve this."

Rachel shook her head. "I don't. Out of everyone, I'm the innocent one, the victim. Mr. Winthrop was a pig. I didn't kill him, but he deserved what he got, and now I'm being punished for it."

Tears flooded Rachel's eyes, and she swiped at them. "People are calling me a witch and sending death threats."

Hazel rubbed the area below her neck, trying to ease the ache in her chest. "You've told the police about the threats, right?"

"Yeah." She turned her gaze back to the window. "They can't protect me, and they won't let me leave town until the murder is solved."

"So, it is a murder investigation, then." Peter had told her as much, but she didn't want to give Rachel that information.

"Apparently." She faced Hazel. "Would you like a list of people besides me who'd wanted him dead? Mick for one. Mr. Winthrop was always on him about something. Mrs. Jones. His wife, for sure. I'm not sure who should hate him more, her or me."

Hazel tilted her head. "For being Mr. Winthrop's lover, you don't seem to like him very much."

Rachel banged a balled fist on the table hard enough to make Hazel jump. "Oh. My. God. Are you serious? People think I was his lover?"

Hazel blinked, so not prepared for that outburst. How did she say this delicately? "Uh...I don't mean to belabor an obviously sore point, but you were found naked with him when he died."

Hatred-filled eyes stared at her, and Rachel leaned closer. "He forced me to have sex with him."

"*Rape?*" Hazel could barely get the word out.

Rachel's anger dropped a notch, and she folded her arms as though that would protect her. "Practically. He...he...my brother owed him a lot of money, and he threatened to have him killed if my brother didn't pay immediately." She paused to take a shaky breath.

Rachel waved an angry hand toward the front room. "Of course, he didn't have it. You've seen him. So, Mr. Winthrop offered an alternative form of repayment."

"He'd forgive your brother's debt if you'd sleep with him," she said quietly.

Rachel sniffed. "It didn't start that way. At first, he'd said I could come work for him at his big house. It seemed like a great opportunity, but I was there less than a month when he started demanding more than cleaning services."

Hazel had sensed the ugliness inside Winthrop from the moment she'd encountered him.

"Does Chief Parrish know about this?"

"Are you kidding? They already think I'm guilty of killing him with witchcraft. If they discover I have a motive to go along with it, you might as well burn me at the stake here and now."

Her chin quivered as she eyed Hazel. "Everyone is questioning me, but did no one stop to wonder why I'd have sex with an old man like him? No. Because he was prominent in the community, they've already convicted me."

Hazel was grateful for the lead in to her pressing question. "First Rachel. I don't think you killed Mr. Winthrop."

Rachel met her gaze with hopeful eyes. "You don't?"

She shook her head. "I'm a pretty good judge of people, and you don't seem like the murdering kind."

Tears filled her eyes again. "Thank you. Besides my brother, you might be the only friend I have in Stonebridge."

"I'll help however I can. Could you tell me more about this witchcraft you've been accused of?"

Rachel lifted her cell phone, tapped it a few times and then pushed it toward Hazel. A screen decorated with candelabras proclaimed to offer any spell a person could want.

"You tried a spell from a website?" Any good witch would tell you they were all fake, because any witch worth her cauldron did not give up the secrets from her book of spells to just anyone. It could put him or her at great risk.

"I told him it was an impotence cure that would help so he wouldn't have to take Viagra all the time. Really, it was supposed to make him less frisky, so he'd leave me alone. Needless to say, it didn't work."

Of course, it didn't. "I'm sorry." She truly meant that. Rachel was the true victim here.

Hazel paused for a moment while she formulated her thoughts. "So, how exactly did the police find out about the spell casting? Mr. Winthrop obviously couldn't tell."

Rachel shrugged. "Maybe Mick? He was always places where he didn't belong. One time I caught him watching me and Mr. Winthrop. He spied on everyone all the time. Maybe he heard us trying the spell or something."

Hazel nodded. "Maybe so." If she had the opportunity, she'd inquire more about Mick when she visited Mrs. Winthrop later that day.

"Also," Hazel added. "You mentioned Mrs. Jones might wish Mr. Winthrop dead. Why would you think that?"

"I found out a few days ago that he did the same thing to her younger sister as he did to me. She committed suicide to end her suffering."

That seemed like a heck of a lot more motive than Rachel had.

"Well, there certainly are a number of people to consider. Chief Parrish is somewhat of a friend of mine." Though how much, she wasn't sure. "I might stop and have a word with him and let him know about what you've told me."

She shook her head. "Don't bother. It won't help."

And he'd already convicted Rachel because he thought she was a witch. Anger welled inside her. She'd obviously overestimated the kindness in that man.

He had a beautiful aura, but apparently, he hid his true self very well like some people could do. She supposed that made for a fine quality in a chief.

But not much of one in a friend.

Hazel pushed her care package toward Rachel. "I should probably be on my way since I have other deliveries to make, but I hope you enjoy these."

Rachel gave her a watery smile. "I'm sure I will." She reached over and wrapped her fingers around Hazel's hand. "Thank you for stopping and thank you for listening. It helps more than you know."

Hazel squeezed her hand, noting the genuine warmth flowing between them. "I'm glad. I'll stop by again in a few days and see if you need anything."

"Don't. I won't be here."

Her thoughts immediately jumped to what Mrs. Jones's sister had done to end her suffering. "You're not going to do anything stupid."

"No," she whispered. "Darrell is getting me out of here on Sunday. He has friends coming in to help, and we're leaving even if we have to shoot everyone who might try to stand in our way."

Her words didn't ease Hazel's apprehension. "That sounds very dangerous."

"Don't worry, sweet Hazel. We're planning to sneak out. The guns are only in case something goes wrong."

How could she think about trying to stop her? Hazel had recently had similar thoughts of running when she'd thought she might be found out.

"Be safe then. I'll be happy when the only gossip I hear is that you managed to escape."

A genuine smile curved Rachel's lips. "Thank you. I'll always remember your kindness."

As Hazel left the rotting house, she couldn't help but be hopeful for Rachel, despite the awful churning in her stomach.

CHAPTER TWELVE

Hazel unlocked her shop Monday morning with a somber shadow hovering over her, much like the clouds that had rolled in during the night. A light mist shrouded their little town, leaving everything damp and gloomy.

She'd stayed up way too late glancing through Clarabelle's book of spells. The original effects of it on her had dissipated, but her hesitancy remained. Some spells were familiar, things she'd learned from her mother. Some made no sense at all.

She'd found a simple one that intrigued her, and she'd garnered enough courage to try it out. They were her family's spells after all, and the glamour one guaranteed to grow her eyelashes longer seemed innocent enough.

Except she'd misread it and used a dark blue candle instead of a black one. Her lashes hadn't grown longer, but luckily, it hadn't cast any other effect on her.

And then there were other malevolent spells that left her shivering. Those ones seemed experimental because many ingredients had been scratched out and replaced by others.

She couldn't believe Clarabelle had been a bad person. That idea didn't fit at all with the entity she'd encountered at the abandoned house. Perhaps she'd tried to create those spells for protection?

After that, Hazel had tossed and turned all night, imagining what Clarabelle and her family had gone through years ago. She alternated that with worrying about Rachel. She hadn't heard a

82

blaze of gunfire or sirens during the wee hours and hoped that was a good sign.

Even so, her mood hadn't improved by the time Gretta arrived an hour later.

Her assistant's demeanor was a different story, all bubbly and smiles, carrying two to-go cups of coffee from Cora's as she came in. "Is it a sin to drink coffee in a teashop?" She grinned.

Hazel eyed her friend, her offering, and then really did smile. "Probably, but we won't tell anyone."

They shared a laugh, and Hazel absconded with the sugar and cream from her tea station. "I really needed a strong dose of caffeine this morning, and tea wasn't cutting it. This is perfect."

"Bad night?" Gretta skipped the extras and went for straight black coffee.

Hazel sipped, letting the hot liquid singe her throat and give her a little kick in the pants. "I couldn't sleep. I think I finally dozed about an hour before my alarm went off."

"Apparently, you weren't the only one."

A sick feeling gripped Hazel's stomach. "You, too?" she asked innocently.

"Not me. Rachel Parker skipped town during the night."

"What?" She did her best to appear surprised. "How do you know?"

"Heard it at the café. Her brother's truck wasn't in the driveway like it always is, so someone knocked on the door. When no one answered, an officer busted in for a welfare check. They were both long gone."

And safe.

She silently thanked the Blessed Mother. "That is crazy. I saw her a few days ago when I stopped by and wouldn't have guessed that's what she was planning." Which was true. She never would have guessed.

Still, Hazel decided it was best to come clean about her visit in advance because someone had likely noticed her car, and questions would certainly come her way.

Gretta widened her eyes as though Hazel was out of her mind. "Why in heaven's name would you ever do that?"

Hazel shrugged. "Curiosity. We'd met at the Winthrop house, and I wanted to see if I could tell if she was a witch."

"And..." Gretta stepped closer, obviously interested.

She laughed, trying to lighten the mood. "I didn't notice anything weird at her house, and she didn't say anything. How do people know that she is?"

Gretta's gaze turned serious. "She did witchcraft with Mr. Winthrop, and now he's dead. If that wasn't damning enough, she has now run from the authorities."

"Maybe she was just scared of being wrongfully accused."

Her assistant eyed her curiously. "Is that what you believe?"

She shrugged again. "I don't know. She did tell me a few things that make others in the Winthrop house seem suspicious. Did you know that Mr. Winthrop blackmailed her into having sex to repay a debt her brother owed?"

Gretta waved off her statement with a flick of her hand. "Between Mr. Winthrop, an outstanding member of our society, and that white trash, I'd have to say she's the guilty one, not him."

"He was found having sex with her when he died," Hazel countered. That alone made him guilty of a sin.

"She could have put a spell on him, coerced him into cheating on his wife. It wouldn't be the first time it's happened in this town."

Wow. Hazel bit her tongue to stop her next argument. She couldn't appear to be too much in Rachel's favor, or it would put her at risk.

Gretta had obviously drunk too much of the town's tainted water and had bought into their fears. To argue against her now would be a mistake.

Instead, she sighed and sipped her coffee. "You may be right."

Gretta studied her for a long moment, enough that Hazel fretted she'd given something away. "New makeup?" Gretta asked instead.

She shook her head and smiled. "No, just my same old boring routine."

"Your eyes seem different."

Hazel shook her head in response and wondered if the spell had worked after all. Maybe the wrong candle only delayed the action.

She brightened with a smile. "I know. We should head into Boston one Sunday and hit Sephora. Their makeup selection is incredible, and I feel like I'm in a candy shop."

"Sounds fun," Hazel said, grateful they'd moved onto a different topic.

They finished their drinks, and then together, they restocked shelves. Hazel gathered more tea for Florence Winthrop. She suspected the request was a ploy to get her to visit again, but Hazel understood Florence's need for people to be around to distract and help her. She didn't mind.

"Are you sure you don't want me to go out? You're still limping, and I could entertain Florence for a while," Gretta offered with a kind smile.

Stuff like that drove Hazel crazy. People in her town could be so sweet, but the dark side lingered like a dormant disease, ready to strike at any time.

"I'm sure. I promised Mrs. Winthrop I'd stay for a longer visit, and I only have the police department and June Stoker besides her. I can rest my foot at Mrs. Winthrop's and the others will be easy-peasy."

"Easy-peasy?" Gretta laughed. "Now you sound like Chief Parrish. You'd better stop spending so much time with him, or people will start talking."

Heat rushed up her cheeks. "What are you talking about? I haven't been spending time with him."

"A couple of people said they saw him outside your house the other night."

She widened her eyes into innocent ovals. "Because he gave me a lift home after I crashed my bike and twisted my ankle. That's it."

"Okay, okay," she mocked. "I think thou doth protest too much." She narrowed her gaze. "Wait. Did you put on lipgloss?"

Hazel rolled her eyes. "I'm leaving before you drive me insane. Try not to cause too much trouble while I'm gone."

"Yes, ma'am," Gretta said with a teasing smile.

Hazel was much more grateful for the chilly temperatures when she stepped outside as opposed to the morning when she'd arrived. The mist cooled her blood and restored the energy she'd lost while trying to maintain the façade with Gretta.

Blessed Mother, it was work living in Stonebridge.

She left a nice-sized package of fresh oolong tea with June Stoker's maid, before she headed back toward town and the police department.

Her old Honda fit perfectly in the tight space between two oversized pickup trucks in front of the historic courthouse. Though the building was more than a century old, the gray rock appeared sturdier than many newer structures she'd seen. The ivy climbing from the gardens at its base added to the charm.

She inhaled a steadying breath before she gathered her deliveries for this stop and exited her car. She would need whatever help she could to remain calm if Chief Parrish was in the vicinity.

Margaret smiled when Hazel approached her desk. "Well, hello there, Miss Hazel. Looks like you've brought just what I need."

Hazel eyed the chief's assistant and her lime green business suit with lavender trim but kept her chuckle to herself. "I'm so happy you love it."

Margaret leaned forward in her seat. "The chief is as big a fan as I am," she whispered conspiratorially.

"I heard that," Peter said from behind them, and Hazel startled.

Part of her had hoped she could drop off the delivery unnoticed. But there was another more reckless side that would have been deeply disappointed if she hadn't caught sight of him.

She turned and worked to keep her composure despite his devastating smile. "Hello, Chief Parrish."

"Hello, Miss Hardy." He moved from the doorway of his office and joined her in front of Margaret's desk. "If you have a few moments, I have more questions for you."

She lifted her brows. "Of course. However, I can help." He wasn't using that as an excuse to get her alone in his office, was he? Not right in front of Margaret. The rumor mill would catch like wildfire and beat her back to her teashop.

"Regarding Rachel Parker and the Winthrop case. You were seen at her house on Friday, correct?"

Whatever vestiges of calmness she'd managed to keep evaporated. "Yes, I stopped by."

"If you haven't heard, Rachel skipped town."

She nodded. "Yes, I'd heard. I'm happy to tell you what I can, but it's not much. I only dropped off tea."

He nodded toward his office. "Then, if you wouldn't mind."

Margaret winked at her as she passed. The gesture didn't help alleviate any of her fears.

Chief Parrish stood near his doorway and lifted a hand, indicating she should enter before him. Once she did, he followed and closed the door, setting off all kinds of crazy alarms inside her.

The shades to his office were drawn, and suddenly, they were in a confined space once again, and Hazel's pulse raced like a hexed man trying to outrun his curse.

He pulled a chair closer to his desk. "Have a seat, please."

She sat, doing her best to maintain her composure.

He released a sigh, obviously not thrilled they were having this discussion, and he pulled out a yellow notepad. When he had his pen ready, he glanced up.

He opened his mouth to speak but stopped. Then he leaned forward ever so slightly. "Your eyes are different."

Panic flared. "Different?" Her lashes must have grown. She'd meant to check before she left the shop but forgot. She glanced upward as though that would help her see what he saw.

"Different color. They're normally brown. Right now, they look like they have a purplish tint."

Blessed Mother, what had she done? "Contact lenses. Purple. I didn't think anyone would notice." Did they even make purple lenses?

He stared at her for a long moment. "I notice everything."

She shivered. That could be a good thing or a very bad one. "A good quality for a police chief, I would say."

"Mmm..." he mumbled and then cleared his throat. "Okay, then. Business. What time did you visit Miss Parker on Friday?"

"She didn't do it, Peter." She knew she'd gone out on a limb by saying so, but playing these ridiculous games while a murderer roamed free bordered on crazy.

"That doesn't answer my question."

She crossed her arms in a defiant gesture. "No, but it does answer the question you should be asking."

A hint of a smile crossed his face, and he leaned back in his chair. "Okay, then. Why don't you tell me how I should run this investigation?"

Her cheeks burned, but she didn't fold. "First off, you should consider all the suspects. Did you know that Mr. Winthrop was blackmailing Rachel Parker, forcing her to sleep with him? And if you give me the she-hexed-him crap, I might scream."

He drew his brows into a frown. "No. I wasn't aware of that." He shifted in his seat. "You do realize that only makes her look guiltier."

"Yes, I am aware, which is also why she didn't come forward with that information." Hazel wouldn't have said a word, either, if Rachel hadn't disappeared.

"Did you know that he did the same to Mrs. Jones's younger sister, and then she committed suicide?"

He scribbled notes on his paper and then met her gaze. "Did you know that Renee Jones practiced witchcraft on a regular basis before she committed suicide?"

Hazel dropped her face into her hands and growled in frustration. What were these women playing at? They knew the town's dangerous bias against witches and what their actions could cost them. They didn't have the lineage or the training to protect themselves. Why would they play with fire?

She faced him. "Look, I realize I'm a newcomer to town, but I don't buy into all this 'witchcraft causes every bad thing that happens' attitude. Rachel Parker wasn't any more of a witch than you are. I doubt Renee Jones was either."

Chief Parrish studied her for a long moment. "Anything else you'd like to add before you answer my questions?"

She huffed. "Rachel also told me that Mick Ramsey liked to spy on her and Mr. Winthrop, and that she'd caught him once watching them having sex."

He raised his brows in interest. "Is that so?" He jotted down more information. With a sigh, he regarded her again. "It seems that you've garnered quite a bit more information from Ms. Parker than she told me."

His statement carried an accusatory tone that she didn't like. She leaned forward and placed her hands on his desk. "That's what happens when you develop trust by listening instead of accusing before you have all the facts. I just asked questions and let her tell me what she wanted."

Instead of taking offense to her words, he smiled. "You are an interesting lady, Miss Hardy. I admire your honesty."

His words knocked her thoughts completely off track, confusing and charming her at the same time. Neither of which sat well with her.

She stood. "I've told you what I know, and I should go. I need to get back to my shop."

He stood as well. As she reached for the doorknob, he caught her elbow and stopped her. "Just so you know, I did not accuse Rachel of anything. I merely asked her questions just as you did. The problem is there are those who believe certain things about my office that simply aren't true. In a way, I've also been judged without others researching all the facts."

He turned the knob and opened the door for her. "Have a nice day, Miss Hardy."

Dumbfounded, she stepped into the outer office and then glanced back at him. "Same to you, Chief Parrish."

CHAPTER THIRTEEN

By the time Hazel visited Florence again, several days had passed and her purple eyes had faded back to brown. Thank goodness it wasn't a permanent spell. Few glamour spells were, but still.

She had promised Florence she would come more often, but her sprained ankle would have made traversing the large staircase painful. She had sent her condolences, knowing the older lady would miss her company, but that couldn't be helped.

Hazel parked her car in the large driveway and smiled. She'd missed her friend and would be happy to see her today. She hoped the poor lady was faring okay.

Inside the kitchen, Mrs. Jones greeted her with her usual grunt. Hazel ached to ask about her sister but knew that was a subject better left in the past.

"Good morning," she greeted the waspish older woman, trying to raise good vibrations in the room.

"You're late again," she said without bothering to look at Hazel.

"Late? What's late?" Hazel said before she could control her mouth. "I make deliveries and can't give an exact time that I'll arrive. You don't need to boil water for me. I'm perfectly capable."

Mrs. Jones nailed her with an annoyed look. "No one—"

"Touches my kitchen. I know. But cut me a little slack, okay?" Her sass surprised even her, but she'd been on edge since her last meeting with Peter.

The cook eyed her for a long moment, and Hazel was sure she was in for a verbal lashing.

"Take that package to Mrs. Winthrop when you go." Mrs. Jones nodded to a fat golden envelope sitting on the edge of the counter. "It came in the mail a few minutes ago, and she's been waiting for it."

"I hope it's her supplements." Hazel said.

"The contents are none of my business," she said, hinting they were also none of Hazel's.

With an exasperated sigh, Hazel finished putting together the tea service and headed toward Florence's bedroom.

"She's in the parlor," Mrs. Jones called after her.

Hazel switched directions and headed toward the room where she'd found Florence and Peter on a previous visit.

She entered and found Florence with her head back on the chair and her eyes closed. She hated to wake the sleeping woman, but she knew Florence would be deeply disappointed if she missed their teatime.

"Hello," she said softly.

The older woman lifted her eyelids and smiled. "There you are. I was just resting for a moment."

"Are you feeling okay?"

Florence grimaced as she shifted in her chair until she was sitting upright. "As well as can be expected, I suppose."

Hazel set down the tray and pulled the golden envelope from beneath her arm. Florence's expression brightened. "Finally! Next time I'll order much further in advance so that I don't have to go without them."

Hazel handed the package over and then poured hot water into their cups. "Today, I brought chamomile in case you need extra rest, or a fun, new hibiscus tea I'm trying that should give you energy. Which would you prefer?"

"I'm tired of sleeping. How about some energy?" Florence said as she tore open the package and dumped a small brown bottle into her hands. "Would you mind fetching a glass of water and a teaspoon from the kitchen, so I can take this, too? Mrs. Jones will know what I need."

"Of course." Hazel filled tea strainers, dropped them into cups of hot water and went to collect the requested items.

Mrs. Jones was none friendlier, but she didn't complain either. As surly as she could be where Hazel was concerned, she seemed quite devoted to the mistress of the house.

Hazel sank onto the old-fashioned brown settee while Florence unscrewed the cap on the bottle and dipped the tiny teaspoon inside.

"Can I ask you a personal question, Florence, about your husband? About his affair?" she added in a softer voice.

The woman met her gaze, wariness in her eyes. "You may ask."

This wasn't a question she could ask gently, so she'd be direct. "Was Rachel your husband's first indiscretion in your marriage that you were aware of?"

The flicker of pain on Florence's face was answer enough. She turned her gaze away. "There were others," she said quietly. "When a man is unable to have relations with his wife, it happens."

Unable to have relations? Obviously, Mr. Winthrop had fixed his troubles regarding sex with a little blue pill, and Florence had expressed a desire to garner her husband's interest when she and Hazel had painted their nails. She couldn't imagine what might be their problem.

Hazel released a sad sigh. "You're more understanding than I would be in that situation."

Florence cursed under her breath and caught Hazel by surprise. "It's not so much that I'm understanding, but what could I have done about it? Leave him? In a town this small and repressed, life would be unbearable after a divorce."

Hazel was glad she wasn't the only one to admit Stonebridge had its share of troubles.

"I could have left town, but this is my home, and I love it here. This is where my friends are, where I'm comfortable. I'm not in a position to pack up and start over somewhere new. So, I turned a blind eye to his affairs. If that makes me a pathetic, silly... woman, then so be it. When you've walked in my shoes, then you can judge."

Hazel put a hand to her mouth as the woman's anguish washed through her. "Oh, Florence. I'm not judging you. I completely understand why you'd want to stay, and I didn't mean to upset you. I just wish they'd find the murderer and put this whole mess to rest. After everything you've been through, you deserve that."

Florence nodded as tears filled her eyes. "It's been more than anyone should have to bear. Losing him was bad enough. Even if he wasn't the best husband."

"Of course, it has."

Hazel switched the subject to the upcoming spring festival while they sipped their tea, filling the older woman in on all the latest, harmless gossip floating around town. She omitted any reference to Rachel or her disappearance. If someone else wanted to upset Florence with that news, they could.

Thirty minutes later, a knock startled them both and drew their gazes.

A tall, lean man about Mrs. Winthrop's age stood at the entrance to the parlor with a questioning look on his kind face. "Florence? Is this a bad time?"

A smile as warm as the sun blossomed on Florence's face. "*Teddy.*" She held out both hands as the man entered the room, walking with a limp.

He wrapped his fingers around hers and kissed both of her cheeks. "So good to see you. I was sorry to hear the news. Are you okay? Anything I can do?"

She sniffed though still smiling and shook her head. "I'd like to introduce you to Hazel Hardy. She owns the new teashop in town and has been a good friend to me. Hazel, this is Theodore Cornaby, a long-time friend and Stonebridge resident."

Hazel shook his hand. "Nice to meet you, Mr. Cornaby."

"Teddy," he countered.

"Teddy, then." She returned his smile. "You live here in town?" She'd thought she'd at least heard of, if not met, everyone in Stonebridge.

"On Vine Street. I'm out of town frequently."

Hazel wanted to ask about another certain house near Vine on Hemlock and its former owners but held her tongue.

"He owns a large, very successful conglomerate company. Isn't that what you call it?" Florence glanced at her friend, obviously pleased with his success.

He seemed embarrassed by her flattery. "Yes, Florence. I've done well with my once small-time business. But I'm not here to talk about me. When I heard the news about Albert, I came straight away."

"Thank you, Teddy. You've always been such a dear friend to me."

The scene warmed Hazel's heart. No one could mistake the affection between these two friends. "Have you known each other a long time?" she asked.

They looked at each other and smiled. "Since we were both youngsters," Teddy answered. "In fact, in high school, I was so smitten I asked her to marry me."

He chuckled. "She, of course, turned me down, which she should have. But we've never doubted we were meant to be friends."

"It's true, Teddy. You've always been dear to me."

Hazel couldn't help but think Florence might have been better off if she'd stuck with Teddy instead of falling for the nasty Mr. Winthrop. "I should go and let you visit."

"Thank you for coming, dear," Florence said. "You're always a bright spot in my day."

"Of course." She sent the older woman a warm smile and then turned to her friend. "Very nice to meet you, Teddy. I hope we will run in to each other again soon."

"Same here, Hazel. Any friend of Florence's is a friend of mine."

CHAPTER FOURTEEN

Gossip about poor Rachel Parker was all Hazel heard as she made her way through the aisles at the local grocery store after closing her shop for the day. It seemed the former maid and mistress of Albert Winthrop had been tried and convicted in the town's eyes without any real evidence or a chance for her day in court.

Thank the Blessed Mother that Rachel had escaped this crazy town. Hazel hoped Rachel would be able to stay in hiding until authorities found the real murderer, and then, perhaps, she would go on to have a good life. That night when Hazel meditated, she'd send positive thoughts her way.

The clerk at the checkout counter was friendly as usual, but Hazel couldn't help thinking how quickly that would change if someone accused her of forbidden activities. Which, she noted, she was actually guilty of, even if the town didn't understand the nature of her spiritual practice.

Before she'd come to Stonebridge, she'd only spent a few hours researching what the town had put online. It seemed like a beautiful place with a bit of unusual history. In her naiveté, she had hoped to come and little-by-little, change the remnants of the town's perceptions of her kind and help them see what it really meant to be a witch.

At least what it meant to be a good witch. Both kinds existed in the world, but the good far outweighed the bad. Not only that, but she and her relatives did their part to help keep the bad in check.

Thoughts of Clarabelle's questionable spells crept into her mind. Then again, there were always shades of gray. Maybe Clarabelle had done things she shouldn't have. But one had to consider her reasons as well.

Hazel had her head down, focused on her deep thoughts as she exited the grocery store into the darkness and chill of early evening.

"Whoa," a deep, far-too-familiar voice said, bringing her gaze up sharply. Peter's hands caught her shoulders a second before she would have plowed into him. "Earth to Hazel," he said with a chuckle.

"Sorry. I should have been paying attention." She took a step back, creating a safer distance between them.

"Don't worry about it. I got your back."

Unless he learned of her heritage. If that happened, she had a sinking feeling he might have her neck instead. "Thanks."

"Let me help you with those bags." Before she could respond, he slid his hands between her stomach and the brown paper bags and pulled them from her. If she'd resisted, her actions would likely result in the bag tearing and freeing oranges to roll unfettered across the parking lot.

"Uh...thanks." She sometimes wished the man wasn't so helpful. The last time they'd been together in public had generated more than enough talk. This could only add to it.

"I haven't seen you for a few days," he said as they walked toward her car.

"Are you supposed to see me every day?" Her comment came out snarky, and she was immediately sorry. Just because he flustered her didn't mean he deserved her rudeness.

"No," he admitted. "But I don't mind it when I do."

She pushed the button on her key fob, and her trunk popped open. He set her bags inside and closed it with a loud whoosh.

"Thanks again." She gave him a quick smile and turned toward the driver's door.

"How are things going?" he asked, not dissuaded by an obvious brush off.

She let her fingers slide off the door handle in dismay and turned back to him. "Good, I suppose. Ankle is feeling much better."

"That's good to hear. Anything else you've heard regarding Mr. Winthrop?" He asked his question so casually that it caught her attention.

Inside, she smiled. He wanted information but didn't want to admit she might be a better sleuth than he was this time.

She leaned back against her car, now enjoying their interlude. "No, not really. I did meet one of Mrs. Winthrop's old friends today. Theodore Cornaby? Nice man."

Chief Parrish leaned next to her, close enough she swore she could feel his body heat. "Ah, Teddy. The man who's pined after Florence for fifty years."

She couldn't help but laugh. "Poor guy. They seemed like good friends, but you think he's still in love with her?"

The chief gave her a friendly nudge with his elbow. "Did you not notice how he looked at her?" he said as though he'd one-upped her sleuthing skills that time.

Her pride bristled. "Maybe." She thought back to the exchange earlier in the day. "Both of them were awfully happy to see each other. I thought it was just friendly, but..." She supposed the emotions she'd sensed could have been more than friendship.

"In all these years, he's never married or had children. But, he's always remained close to Florence. I recall one town festival when Albert Winthrop was out of town. She attended, which is rare, and if memory serves me, she and Teddy spent a considerable amount of time together throughout the evening. Not enough to cause gossip, but if one looked close enough..."

An outrageous, but possible scenario popped into her mind, and she turned to face him. "Are you suggesting that perhaps he and Florence have also had a love affair all these years?"

He narrowed his gaze as he considered her suggestion. "No, she seemed pretty devoted to her husband, even if he didn't deserve it. But I'm not sure Teddy ever got over her."

She opened her palms outward. "Then there's another suspect for you to investigate. With Mr. Winthrop out of the picture, Teddy might have thought he'd have another chance."

She released an exasperated sigh. "Except he'd mentioned today that he'd been out of town, so that eliminates him."

"Unless he lied," the chief countered. "I'll check to see if he has a solid alibi. Then we can eliminate him if he does."

He leaned away from the car and trapped her with his gaze. "Thanks for listening. You're good at helping me think and process ideas."

She blushed at his compliment. "Of course. You're welcome."

"We should have dinner sometime."

His statement struck an equal mixture of fear and excitement into her heart. "Oh. I don't know if that's a good idea."

He tilted his head. "Why not?"

She wrapped her arms about her to ward off the chill of the night. "People are already gossiping about us, speculating on a relationship. Dinner would only fuel that fire."

He paused and seemed to consider her words. "So, does next week work for you?"

Her mouth dropped open. "Didn't you hear what I said?"

"Yeah. I did. I can't see why that's a problem, though." He graced her with a heart-melting smile. "Think about it. I'll check with you later," he said over his shoulder as he walked away.

Hazel climbed into her car, still processing their conversation. Hadn't she turned him down? She swore she had, but then why was he leaving her to think about it?

She briefly closed her eyes and shook her head. "Blessed Mother, please send strength and patience to me. I'm going to need all I can get."

CHAPTER FIFTEEN

Hazel blended batches of herbs into tea in the backroom of the shop while Gretta tended the front. Snippets of information collided in her brain as she tried to piece together the murder.

Over the past few days, she'd puzzled over the chief's suspicions regarding Teddy and Florence. Had they ever been more than friends back before she'd married? Were they more than friends now?

It didn't help that she'd found Teddy at Florence's house again the last time she'd delivered tea, which ramped up her concerns a hundred percent.

Rachel had been with Mr. Winthrop when he died, but Hazel didn't believe she was guilty. Mrs. Jones certainly had cause to want him dead. After all, he'd been the reason her sister had taken her own life.

She had her suspicions about Mick, but she couldn't see that there was any real evidence against him other than he was a voyeuristic creep. As far as she could tell, he'd gained nothing by Mr. Winthrop's death.

Then there was Teddy, the jilted lover. He seemed like a kind man, and she hadn't gotten any malicious vibes from him when he'd been near. That could be because he didn't consider her a threat or because he wasn't guilty.

Frustrated, she scooped the contents of her current creation into bags and tied them off.

Earlier that week, Gretta had noted that the summer season would be upon them soon, and they'd garner an influx of tourists wanting to experience a former witch town. Tea was likely to be a highly sought-after witch-like commodity, especially if she labeled them with catchy titles.

Hazel had expressed concern that she didn't want others in town to question if she was a witch. Gretta had assured her that she'd passed the non-witch test months ago and that citizens of Stonebridge loved her.

Here she was a witch incognito, acting like a person who was pretending to be a witch, when really, she was the opposite. Talk about messed up.

She sighed and stuck labels on tins for this batch. Love Potion #29. Drinking it would increase the chances of finding love before Valentine's Day the following year.

She mentally shrugged. It wasn't necessarily a lie. Her concoction had worked on a friend in high school. Maybe it would work for others, too. Either way, it was a very sweet smelling, tasty tea, sure to please a lover's palate.

When she finished, she gathered the five tins she'd just filled and hauled them out to the main room where she'd set up a special Witch's Brew section and stacked them next to Heebie Jeebies Tea that promised to ward off bad spirits.

"What does that one do?" Gretta asked from behind the counter.

Hazel turned and grinned. "It's a love potion." She widened her eyes as though that made it more secret and potent.

They both laughed.

"Seriously, though. You watch," Gretta said. "You'll see an uptick in sales."

Hazel straightened tins on the shelf and then crossed to where her employee stood at the counter. "I'm surprised the town goes for that sort of thing. They seem pretty against anything to do with witches."

Gretta grinned and shook her head as though Hazel's response was the silliest thing she'd heard all day. "Yes, but this is all for fun. It isn't real."

"Of course," Hazel agreed. "That makes all the difference."

She paused for a few beats and then plowed forward with the subject that had been on her mind all morning. "You know Teddy Cornaby, right?"

"Sure." Gretta squirted cleaner on the glass counter and wiped. "He's a very nice man."

"He has been at Mrs. Winthrop's the last two times I've visited, and she's been very happy to have him there. Last time, I even felt as though they were in a hurry for me to leave, as though I was cramping their style. This is purely speculative, and I don't want to start any gossip, but I wondered if you thought maybe their relationship could be more than friends."

Gretta pondered for a few moments and then nodded. "Maybe. Yes, I could see where it could be a possibility. He is very protective of her. And, you know, there was this one time I remember very clearly that he took a swing at Mr. Winthrop."

Hazel widened her eyes in interest. "Tell me more." If she was going to encourage gossip, she might as well use it in her favor.

Gretta scrunched her features as though that would help her access her memory. "It was at a public function, maybe a year ago. A dinner and silent auction to benefit the library. Mrs. Winthrop attended, which she doesn't usually because of her ailments. In place of Mr. Winthrop, if I recall. I remember her apologizing for his absence, but she was there in his place.

"It was a lovely event held during the summer under the stars," she continued. "Everyone dressed so fancy. Mrs. Winthrop seemed to be on top of her game, having a fantastic evening. I do recall that she'd danced with Teddy Cornaby several times, and she always looked flushed when he returned her to the table next to my family's. It was good to see her so happy."

"But Mr. Winthrop showed up."

"That's right. The evening was almost at an end when Mr. Winthrop arrived. Mrs. Winthrop and Teddy had danced not long before, but this time, instead of bringing her back to her table, they stood at the edge of the dancefloor talking. Mr. Winthrop took exception to someone chatting up his wife in his absence, and the men exchanged several heated words before Mrs. Winthrop stomped off, red-faced and looking mortified. Teddy balled a fist, but someone...I don't remember who held him back long enough for Mr. Winthrop to get in the last word and chase after his wife."

Gretta tucked a strand of midnight hair behind her ear. "Most chalked it up to too much drinking, but now that you bring it up again, it does make me wonder exactly how much Teddy cares for her."

Hazel nodded thoughtfully. "I'm starting to think the same. Chief Parrish said he'd check his alibi."

Gretta's expression brightened. "Oh? You've already talked it over with the handsome chief?"

Hazel rolled her eyes. "It wasn't like that. We had a casual conversation while he helped me carry groceries to my car."

"That's very gentlemanly. I don't recall him helping any other ladies in town with their groceries." She placed a pointer finger on her lips and shifted her gaze toward the ceiling as though trying to remember.

"Stop," Hazel chided. "There's nothing between us." Even though she suspected more and more that Peter might wish for there to be.

Her assistant shrugged. "If you say so."

She shook off her annoyance and refocused on the murder. "If you saw this heated display between the two men, then most of the town probably did, too. The chief would already know about this, right?"

"Maybe," Gretta answered. "I don't know how much he pays attention to gossip. Even if he did hear or see it, he may have forgotten."

"Maybe you should pay him a visit and tell him," Hazel suggested.

"Or," Gretta enunciated with exaggeration. "Maybe you should. You're the one he wants to see. Not me."

Hazel sighed. "Just go tell him. You can go now on company time."

She wrinkled her nose and shook her head. "I think you'd better go. That way you can know for sure that he knows because you seem very adamant that happens."

Her attitude pricked Hazel's ire. "Aren't you? A man is dead after all."

"If I didn't think you'd take care of it, I would. But I know you'll do it."

Hazel stared her down for ten long seconds. "You are the worst."

"No, I'm not," she said in her sweetest voice. "I'll man the store while you do what you can to help the handsome chief solve the crime."

If she could hex Gretta's shoelaces and make her trip right then, she would have. "Fine. I'll do my civic duty and tell the chief."

She retrieved her purse from the back room and hoofed it the block and a half to the police station.

Margaret greeted her with a warm smile. "Hey, girlfriend. He's in his office. Go right in."

Hazel paused. "Shouldn't you announce me or something? What if he's busy?"

A conspiratorial smile twinkled in her eyes. "I have a feeling he won't be too busy to see you."

Great. Just great. Now, his assistant was in on the matchmaking.

Hazel's pulse increased with each step she took from the front desk to Peter's office. The door was closed, so she knocked.

"Come in," he called.

She sucked in a steadying breath, hoping it would calm her nerves and opened the door.

"Hazel," he said with a smile. "Come in."

She entered and purposely left the door open. She wasn't about to fuel any of the silly rumors floating about town. She sat in front of him at his desk like she had the previous time, and a mass of butterflies rampaged her stomach.

"You brought me more information." He seemed so certain. And he was right.

"Maybe. Maybe not. Do you remember an auction last year for the library? A night where Mrs. Winthrop attended alone until her husband showed up at the end?"

He leaned back in his seat. A cold chill expanded from him and descended on her senses like a thick fog. "Actually, I was out of town during that time."

"You missed the town's big event?" she asked in a teasing tone, trying to bring the light back into his heart.

He gave one swift nod. "It was the anniversary of my wife's death. I'd traveled to Pennsylvania to return her ashes to her family's burial plot. They'd asked that she be placed there, and I thought she might like to go home."

He snorted sadly. "She always wanted to go home. I should have taken her."

Overwhelming pain shot straight to Hazel's core. Deep grief expanded, and she recognized his love for the woman he'd married.

But she also sensed his acceptance and willingness to continue on in his life and make space in his heart for future happiness. "I'm so sorry, Peter. I...I didn't know."

"No." He released a long breath. "Of course, you didn't. And that's in the past now, where it's best left."

He scrubbed a quick hand over his jaw and met her gaze once again. "You came to give me some news."

Hazel quickly repeated Gretta's story. "Since you weren't in town, you could ask others to corroborate what she said, though I don't think she'd have any reason to lie."

"No, I don't either. And it certainly adds more suspicion to Teddy Cornaby. I think maybe it's time I bring him in for formal questioning."

A shiver raced over her. "I don't want to believe that nice man could be guilty of such a crime, but I guess many people throughout history have done crazy things for love."

"Ain't that the truth?" He tapped his pen as he stared at the yellow pad in front of him, and she sensed the duality fighting inside him. Was he trying to decide if he should also impart more information, or was something else bothering him?

He stopped and met her gaze. "A word of caution. Stay away from Mrs. Jones next time you visit the house."

"Why?"

"She'll likely be in a worse mood than before. With Florence's blessing, I ransacked the kitchen looking for anything that might indicate foul play caused by witchcraft or poison."

She grew silent and very still. For all she knew, there were still remnants of her special sleeping tea in that pantry. "And?" she managed to say.

"Nothing. But we have one angry cook on our hands. I promised Florence I'd have the priest out later today to bless the house, check for residual black magic and to clear it of negative energy."

The priest wouldn't be able to detect the presence of her magic, would he? After all, she hadn't been careful to conceal or protect herself or her works while she'd been inside. If he was a regular priest, she'd have nothing to fear. But there were those in the world who could sense otherworldly things.

Once again, she wondered if she should pack and run like Rachel or take her chances. "I'm sure that will put Florence's mind to rest."

He raised his brows as if to question that topic. "Let's hope so."

Hazel ached to run, but a question kept her glued to her seat. "You mentioned poison. Do you have reason to believe the murderer poisoned Mr. Winthrop?"

"Possibly. The autopsy revealed he died by asphyxiation. Since you all watched him take his last breath, that rules out that he might have been smothered. Poison, something that would keep him from taking in air, is my only other option."

"Or witchcraft," she added, trying to keep the sarcasm from her voice.

"Yes. Witchcraft." He exhaled, sounding frustrated. "One more thing while you're here, Hazel."

Something in his tone put her on alert. "Of course. What is it?"

His gaze, dark and serious, pinned her. "You failed to mention Mr. Winthrop forced you off the drive, causing you to crash your bike as you approached his house the day he died. Mick Ramsey stated you were very angry at the time."

She clenched her jaw, withholding the string of nasty words hovering there. "Of course, I was angry. Wouldn't you be? But I wasn't angry enough to kill the man."

She shifted in her chair. "Are you seriously considering me as a suspect?"

"A bright young woman once suggested that I needed to consider everyone until I could rule them out."

She smirked at his comment. "I don't believe that would hold up in court as a motive for murder unless I was a psychopath who was bent on revenge for a minor infraction. Which obviously, I'm not. Just in case I need to point that out."

He grinned then, and despite her ire, her insides warmed as well. "No worries. You've been ruled out. I was just curious why you'd hide that from me."

"I didn't hide it. I just didn't think about it after everything that had happened that day." Curses on Mick for bringing it up again.

He trapped her with a beguiling gaze. "No more secrets, then?"

Her conscience instantly engaged in battle mode. She'd always prided herself on telling the truth, but how could she now? Not when it might endanger her life. She swallowed, but the lie remained on her tongue. "Of course not. I'm an innocent person."

With only one tiny thing to hide.

"Good."

She stood, taking that as an excellent time to vacate his office. He followed suit and walked her to his door. "Have you given any thought to which day we should go to dinner?"

She bit her bottom lip, wanting so much to say yes. "I really don't think it's a good idea, Chief Parrish."

"Peter," he corrected.

"It's not a good idea, Peter," she repeated.

"I see. You need more time to decide. That's okay. I'm not going anywhere." He placed a hand on the small of her back and guided her toward Margaret's desk. "Thanks for stopping by, Hazel. Feel free to do so any time."

Margaret beamed, leaving Hazel unable to concoct a decent reply. Instead, she smiled. "I guess I'll see you both later."

"Bye," Margaret called.

"Later," Peter said with a promise in his eyes.

CHAPTER SIXTEEN

Hazel was back on her bicycle the following morning, excited to be out in the fresh air. She'd loaded her deliveries into her basket and had climbed on board. As she pedaled, she found herself humming.

Humming.

She never hummed. Not unless she was happy, and she had no reason to feel particularly happy now. Not living on the edge of disaster as she was.

She wasn't sure why she took a different route this morning, one that took her past the police station, but she did. Maybe she'd been avoiding thinking about Peter. And maybe she needed to.

She couldn't keep pretending he didn't affect her. Maybe, after this case was solved and she had no reason to see him often, things between them would cool.

She'd have to take in the police station's weekly tea delivery, but she could pop in and out and not stick around. Or perhaps ask Gretta to take theirs and a couple of others, feigning a growing client list that had become hard to manage.

It could happen, she reasoned.

As she neared the police station, a police cruiser pulled to a stop in front of the building. The officer stepped out and then helped an angry Teddy from the backseat.

The promised interrogation. Hazel stopped her bike not far from the doors and pretended to rearrange the contents of her basket.

"You're making a huge mistake," Teddy said as he wrenched his arm free from the officer.

Hazel didn't glance up as they passed a hundred feet away and entered the building. The doors closed behind them and stirred the burning curiosity inside her. She'd give anything to be a fly on the wall.

She glanced at her basket. Maybe she couldn't be a fly, but she could take the sample package of her new Himalayan spiced chai she'd created earlier that week and had intended to give to Mrs. Stoker who loved that sort of thing. She could give it to Margaret instead. If Peter tried it, she knew he'd like it.

Hazel might not hear anything, depending on where Peter conducted his interrogations, but then again, she might learn something.

The prospect of overhearing had her off her bike and walking into the police station. Just as she stepped into the main area, the door to Peter's office closed.

"Hey," she said to Margaret with a bright smile.

"Well, hello, Miss Hazel." Today, Margaret wore all black, from her slick, vinyl pants to the blouse that laced all the way up her neck. She glanced toward Peter's office and then gave Hazel a sad smile.

"Bad timing today. The chief just went in with someone."

"I didn't come to see Chief Parrish," she said with a smug smile. "I came to see you and bring you this."

She offered the package of tea. "As one of my best customers, I wanted you to be the first to try my new spiced chai."

Raised voices came from inside Peter's office, and they both paused to glance in that direction.

"Look," Teddy said in a voice loud enough to penetrate the door. "I did not kill that man. Did he deserve to die? One hundred percent yes. But I didn't kill him."

"Please have a seat, Mr. Cornaby," Peter said in a lowered tone, and Hazel realized just how much Margaret could hear of every conversation that took place in Peter's office. No wonder she thought Peter liked her.

"*Mr. Cornaby? Really? Is that what we've disintegrated to, Chief Parrish.*"

"I have to ask, Teddy. We both know you've loved Florence for a long time. She suffered at the hand of her husband, and maybe you'd had enough and decided it was time to claim her for yourself. That gives you motive to kill. Many would understand."

He snorted. "I didn't kill him. It wouldn't have done me any good, anyway. She doesn't love me like that. I've asked her to run away with me numerous times over the years, but she always turned me down. Perhaps you need to find that witch who escaped town, huh? Why did she run if she didn't do it?"

"Rest assured, Teddy. We're working all angles of the investigation. All I need from you is someone who can vouch for your whereabouts that morning, and I'll cross your name right off that list."

"No, I don't have anyone who can give me an alibi. I was alone in a hotel room in Boston." Teddy said, anger lacing each word.

"That's unfortunate." Hazel could hear in Peter's voice that he really felt it was.

"Am I under arrest then?"

"No. Not now. I intend to continue the investigation, but we will be checking records, purchases, etc. over the past year."

"Do whatever you need to, Chief Parrish. In the meantime, I'll be contacting my lawyers."

A long pause ensued, and Hazel switched her attention back to Margaret, knowing the interrogation would soon be at an end. "Uh...I was saying I'd hoped you'd be willing to try my new blend of chai tea and let me know what you think about it. Then maybe if you like it, you could spread the word."

"Of course." Excitement lit Margaret's eyes as she took the gift. "I would love to be your official taste tester. You just say the word."

She lifted the lid from the tin and sniffed. "Smells amazing. If you want to hang around, I could make us both a cup. It would give you a good excuse to see Chief Parrish."

She cringed as her cursed cheeks heated again. "That's okay. He's busy, and I really did come to see you. I have other deliveries to make, so I'll catch you on Monday for your regular delivery, okay?"

"All right." The flamboyant lady seemed disappointed. "We'll see you then."

Hazel hurried from the building before Teddy, or worse, Peter could discover she'd been in the office and had overheard every word.

She was headed to Florence's next and at complete odds with herself now. Did she warn her friend of Teddy's possible involvement? It would break her heart. But if she was in danger...she had to know.

When Hazel arrived, she found discovering the whereabouts of Florence had become a hide and seek game with nearly every visit it seemed. She certainly ventured out of her bedroom more often these days. Who could blame her though?

Hazel had almost given up searching when she found Florence in her husband's bathroom this time, rifling through his medicine cabinet. Her features were contorted as though she was in pain. "Florence? Are you okay?"

The woman squeaked in surprise and then grimaced. "Lord, but you gave me a fright." She sighed. "This darned hip is acting up something awful today, and I need more ibuprofen. Albert used to keep a bottle in here, but I don't see it, and I didn't think I could make the trek downstairs. I'd like something stronger, but I can't have another pain pill until later today."

"Why don't you go lie down, and I'll ask Mrs. Jones for some for you? You're looking a little peaked and should probably get off your feet. I think I'll grab what's left of the chamomile tea if you'd like to rest this afternoon. It might be good for you." Whatever Hazel didn't use for Florence would be going home with her that afternoon.

Her shoulders slumped in relief, and she gave Hazel a grateful smile. "I'm so lucky that God graced me with friends like you. Thank you so much for being here for me through this ordeal. I don't know what I would have done without you."

Hazel beamed as warmth and goodness spread through her. She loved helping people. "I'll be right back."

She steeled her nerves as she descended the stairs, not wanting to go back into the angry beast's lair once again. The lashing she'd taken the first time around was enough to make a lesser woman cry. But, surprisingly, Mrs. Jones said nothing and quickly located both items along with a glass of water for Hazel and sent her on her way.

The woman was a conundrum. Hopefully, she wasn't a murderer, too. At least Hazel had no reason to think Florence would be in danger from her. Mrs. Jones had hated Mr. Winthrop and saw his wife as a victim, the same as her sister.

"Here we are." Hazel handed two pills and the water to Florence before she set about making her a nice cup of soothing tea.

When she handed her the cup, Florence eyed the tea service. "You're not having some with me?"

"Not this time, I think. Let's just focus on you for now." She tucked the bedcovers tighter against Florence before she dragged the closest chair nearer to the bed.

Thoughts of warning her about Teddy repeated in her head like a squawking crow, but she couldn't bring herself to add more stress to the poor woman. "How has your day been? Any other visitors?"

Florence swallowed. "No. Teddy promised to stop by but hasn't yet. If he does now, he'll just have to come back tomorrow. When you leave, will you let Mrs. Jones know I'm not up for visitors for the rest of the day?"

"Of course." That would give Hazel a little time to decide what to do. As much as she'd hate to ask, maybe Peter could give her some good advice.

"I think I wore myself out going through Albert's papers this morning. That man might have been a lot of things, but organized, he was not."

"I'm happy to come over an afternoon here and there to help if you'd like."

She graced her with a warm smile. "You are always so good to me. If I'd had a daughter, I would wish for her to be just like you."

"You and Mr. Winthrop never had children?" Hazel wasn't aware of any, but that didn't mean they didn't exist.

"No. I miscarried twice, and then was never able to conceive again. I've accepted it now, but there were days when I longed for a child more than anything."

"I'm sorry. That must be hard."

Disappointment lingered with sadness on her features. "I must say my life certainly wasn't what I expected when I'd agreed to marry Albert all those years ago. You make sure when you pick a man that you pick the right one."

Hazel nodded, wondering if she referred to her choice between Albert and Teddy. "I will."

Florence sighed and handed her cup to Hazel. The effects of her special tea were working, and Hazel felt better at seeing relief replace the harsh effects of pain on the poor lady's face. "Rest well," she said and patted her hand.

Within a few moments, deep, restful breaths rumbled from the woman's chest. Hazel stood, proud of a job well done. She might not be a scientist or create machines that could fly a man to the moon, but she helped others, and in her mind, that was just as important.

And no one ever, *ever*, could convince her that using her gifts to enhance her quality of care was a bad thing. Look at the difference between Florence now and when she had arrived.

Satisfied, she dragged the chair back to its original position, pausing when she spied a small, diamond-cut blue pill lying in the divot where one of the chair's legs had rested. She bent to pick it up, examining the slick, shiny surface.

It wasn't one of Florence's. Hazel had helped her take her medicine enough times that she would have remembered that specific color. But then who?

She thought of placing it on the table where they'd often drank tea, but her gut urged her to pocket it instead. Her instincts rarely failed her.

CHAPTER SEVENTEEN

Instead of heading back to the shop, Hazel called Gretta to let her know she'd be a bit longer. Then promptly placed a call to Stonebridge's Chief of Police.

"Hello?" Of course, his voice sounded deeper, more alluring over the phone.

"Peter? It's Hazel. I was wondering if we could meet."

A soft chuckle came from his end. "Decided to take me up on my offer after all?"

His words could have come across as creepy, but they didn't. "No, but I do need to ask you something. I don't want to stop by your office or have you come to my house."

"Eventually, you're going to have to accept that people will talk about us."

She snorted. "There is no us. Now, will you meet me or not?"

"I'm here for whatever you need. Do you have a place in mind?"

There were a lot of remote locations in and around Stonebridge but none that she knew particularly well. She'd always stuck close to the center of town. "How about near that abandoned house on Hemlock? It's a dead end, so I wouldn't expect traffic, would you?"

"No. My officers and I patrol it once or twice a day, but most others avoid that area all together. When?"

"I'm on my bike, so give me fifteen minutes, okay?"

"I'll see you soon, Hazel."

The line went dead, and she tried to shake off the sizzle of excitement he always left her with. This was business. Serious business, and she needed to keep her mind on that.

Hazel arrived before the chief did, and, like before, experienced the incredible peace radiating from the grove of trees along with the compelling pull from the house. She hid her bike as before and walked toward the large mass of maples and pines.

Pinecones and pieces of dried leaves from the previous fall lay scattered across the wild grasses. Columns of sunlight here and there pierce the overhead canopy and created interesting patterns on the ground.

She closed her eyes and breathed in pure energy. It seeped into each pore and cleansed her soul of all the hurt she'd absorbed during the past few weeks along with all the worry she'd created herself. Some called this a tree bath. She called it pure bliss.

A presence entered her senses, and she opened her eyes, expecting Peter had somehow managed to sneak up on her.

But no one was near.

Then, from the corner of her eye, she caught sight of ginger-colored fur a good ten feet away and narrowed her focus on the two intense green eyes staring at her. "Oh, there you are. So, you do have a way in and out of the house."

The beautiful cat continued to stare.

"I still haven't forgiven you." She rubbed her elbow that still ached from time to time.

He flicked his tail as though annoyed but otherwise didn't move.

"I can see that you don't trust me anymore than I trust you, so why don't you just scoot along?" She flicked her fingers at him in encouragement.

The sound of a vehicle approaching drew her attention. Peter. She cast another glance at the cat. "Go," she whispered vehemently.

Of course, he refused.

She turned her back on the stubborn cat and walked closer to the road. Peter greeted her with a warm smile as he emerged from his car, and she found herself returning the gesture.

"I'm glad you called," he said as he joined her. "After the morning I had, I need a pleasant distraction."

So, that's what she was, a pleasant distraction. She weighed the words and deemed them okay. Certainly could be worse, like *the love of his life*.

"Can we walk a little? Into the trees?" she asked.

"You really are worried about being seen. Am I that bad?"

"No," she said before she could stop herself. "I just don't like being the favorite topic of conversation for the day, especially when everything they say is all lies and speculation."

"Lies and speculation, huh?"

She shrugged and began walking. He followed alongside her. She supposed pleasant distraction was a nicer way of putting their so-called relationship, but she wasn't willing to take back her words now.

Instead, she pulled the little blue pill from her pocket and laid it out in her palm. "Do you know what this is? I found it a little while ago in Florence's room. I probably shouldn't be so nosy, but I'm certain it's not hers."

He snorted. "No, that's definitely not hers."

She drew her brows together in confusion.

"It's Viagra. What older men take if they need help in the bedroom."

"Ohhh..." She drew out the word, recalling now the jokes she'd heard when hanging out at a bar near her hometown, and people's references to a blue miracle pill.

Really, she wasn't that naïve.

As her feet crunched leaves and pinecones, she tried to piece together how this find would fit into the puzzle. "I don't get it."

She flicked a glance toward Peter who had his focus on the path ahead. "Florence has made it clear several times that she and Mr. Winthrop haven't shared a marital bed in quite some time. We both know that he did with Rachel at least, but then why would he have his pills in Florence's room?"

Peter remained quiet for a spell, and she guessed he was working with this new bit of information as well. After a few moments, he stopped abruptly.

She did the same and turned to him.

"Maybe it's not Mr. Winthrop's," he said.

Her pulse leapt with the thrill of discovery, and she widened her eyes. "Maybe it belongs to Teddy, and there *is* more than what they're telling."

He grinned. "You're really cute when you get excited over something."

She released an exaggerated groan. "Stop flirting and focus on the topic at hand. This is a murder investigation, remember? A man is dead."

His smile remained in place. "Don't worry. I remember. Viagra. Possibly Teddy and not Mr. Winthrop."

"The question is, how do we find out who it belongs to?"

He nodded toward farther into the woods. "Come on. I know a place we can sit and think. It's not far."

They hiked another quarter of a mile through thick trees. At one point, his fingers brushed hers, and for a second, she thought he'd try to take her hand. But the moment passed with no further action, and she shook off the spark of electricity he'd generated.

Ahead, Hazel spotted a small area that had been cleared of trees, and every sense she had skyrocketed. Her heartbeat kicked in to overdrive without warning, and she gasped.

"Beautiful, huh?" He watched her, and she tried not to overreact, but this was quite literally the most incredible place she'd ever been. Her connection to the Blessed Mother was the strongest she could recall.

"It's breathtaking." To say the least.

Several benches constructed of rock and smooth wood surrounded the outer edges of the clearing. In the center, the remains of what must have been a large bonfire lay charred and lifeless. Tufts of spring grass grew everywhere the sun would reach.

Peter led the way to one of the benches, and they sat.

Without a doubt, her grandmother and several other witches had practiced their craft here. The area vibrated with so much energy. "How did you find this place?"

"My wife and I stumbled upon it one day when out for a walk. It became one of our favorite places to picnic."

"I can see why. It's magnificent."

"And of course, I've been called to the area in recent years because teenagers also discovered it's a great place to have a drinking party. Hence, the big bonfires. The kids should realize they give them away. They think the fires are hidden by trees, but smoke rises."

She chuckled and then sighed. "Kids will be kids."

"Yeah. At least they're harmless." He shifted on the bench so that he faced her. "My gut is telling me it's Teddy."

"Really?" She bounced her heels on the ground, which for some reason helped her to think better. "I want to agree. Things are really pointing at him, but... Can you get access to his medical records? See if he has a prescription?"

Peter rubbed the backs of his fingers across the scruff on his chin. "I'd have to have enough of a compelling reason to convince a judge to issue a warrant. I'd want to search his house, too. My second option is to bring him in again and question him, but after his belligerent attitude this morning, I doubt he'll cooperate now."

"Okay. I'm just going to say this. It's probably nothing, but for whatever reason, it's still floating around in my mind. Maybe because I found this mysterious pill."

She released a breath she hadn't realized she'd been holding. "When I went to visit Florence today, I found her in her husband's bathroom. She had half the bottles from his medicine cabinet sitting by the sink, and she was in the process of removing more. She said she was looking for ibuprofen because of her bad hip, which wouldn't be abnormal for her."

He lifted a shoulder and let it drop. "Then it's probably nothing."

"Probably not." She fought to release the thought. Hated herself for even going down that road, but she couldn't let it go. "But when I went to place the new bottle I'd gotten from Mrs. Jones, I found that she already had some in *her* bathroom."

He studied her for a long moment with amazing green eyes that had fascinating tiny specks of brown in them. "You think Florence may be involved?"

She drew a strand of hair across her lips, rethinking what she'd just said. "No. No, I don't believe she could kill anyone." She tilted her head to the side as thoughts continued to churn. "But there are things that don't make sense."

"Like this pill in her room, and her searching his medicine cabinet." She paused. "You can't overdose on Viagra, can you?"

He snorted. "It can cause...complications, but it won't cause asphyxiation."

She smiled in embarrassment. "So, there's really nothing she could do with them that would hurt him anyway. It's a moot point, and we move on. Back to Teddy."

He lifted a hand. "Not so fast. If she'd somehow coated them with a poisonous substance, she could deliver it that way."

She shook her head. "I really can't see her doing that."

"There's only one way to tell. Besides, even if that's how he was poisoned, it doesn't mean Florence did it. Other people in the house had access. Find his Viagra. At this point, locating his prescription might be easier than checking to see if Teddy has any."

"Wouldn't you have to have a search warrant for that, too?"

His lips turned into a sly grin. "I would, but, say, someone who already has access to the house might be able to do a little checking on the side."

It was her turn to smile. "Is the Chief of Stonebridge asking me to investigate for him? Isn't that illegal or something? Wouldn't the evidence be inadmissible?"

He pressed his lips into a thin line and stared up at the trees while nodding. "If a certain concerned citizen was to find something suspicious in a murder victim's house and look for further evidence, and then present it to the police because she's worried..."

He shrugged and smiled. "All perfectly admissible. You'd have to testify where you found it and why you decided to look. Obviously, you may want to omit this conversation, but..."

She allowed a pleased smile to curve her lips. "It appears there are some in this town who aren't as morally strict as I'd originally thought."

For once, it was his turn to act embarrassed. "Doesn't having the right outcome forgive a little tweaking the truth along the way?"

Yes, they might be friends after all. "It does in my world. Let's go see what we can find."

She glanced at her watch. "Florence will likely sleep most of the afternoon." If her tea was worth what she claimed it to be in other circles. "I'll stop by again, and if anyone questions, I'll say I left something in her room. I'm there often enough that no one will be suspicious."

"Good. Let me know if you find anything."

"Oh, I will. As a concerned citizen, I'll bring it straight to the chief's attention."

"I'll wait until I hear from you before I send this off to the lab for testing. I don't want to make this messier than it needs to be."

They stood and began to retrace their path back to the real world.

One thing still bothered Hazel. "Can I ask a favor, though? If there's nothing that comes of this, can we keep what we've discussed and learned a secret? I don't want to hurt Florence more than she's already been."

"Absolutely."

She smiled. There might be something decent about this man after all.

CHAPTER EIGHTEEN

As Hazel pedaled her way back to the Winthrop house, she altered between wanting to throw up, cry, or head home and not come out of her house for days. What had seemed like a great idea while she and Peter were in the woods, now seemed like betrayal or worse...a witch hunt.

Florence had been nothing but kind to her, and she couldn't picture her hurting anyone. Ever. The only reason Hazel continued her quest was to prove once and for all that the lovely woman was as innocent as she seemed.

In some ways, Hazel was acting just like the crazed citizens from Stonebridge's past, eager to cast blame without regard for the consequences.

Well, that last part wasn't quite true, but she felt like an awful person anyway.

She parked her bike in the usual spot and by-passed Mrs. Jones in the kitchen by entering through the front door. Something she never would have done while Mr. Winthrop was alive.

The stairs creaked as Hazel ascended. At the end of the hall, she opened Florence's door to peek in on her. She found the bed empty and froze. Full-fledged panic flooded her as if Florence had caught her red-handed already.

Blessed Mother, help her.

She worked to steady her mind and took slow, even breaths.

Where had Florence gone? And why wasn't she still asleep?

At least she hadn't caught Hazel. Yet.

She could leave right now and most likely slip out unseen. If someone saw her, she could say she'd been worried about Florence and had returned.

With that settled, she turned to leave.

Then the stupid voice inside reminded her she'd made it this far undetected. She could still take a quick glance around and use the excuse of looking for Florence if anyone found her.

As long as they didn't catch her opening drawers.

For several long moments, she hovered in the hall, listening for any sign that someone else might be on the same floor. Nothing.

With her heart thudding, Hazel sneaked down the hall to where Mr. Winthrop had spent his time. She entered his bedroom and softly closed the door behind her. From there, she walked swiftly to his bedside to check the nightstand for the prescription bottle.

Nothing there.

She searched his dresser, closet, and even under the bed, and came up empty-handed.

A creak that seemed to come from the hall brought her to an abrupt halt. She froze. Her lungs burned for air to compensate for her racing pulse, but she didn't dare breathe for several long seconds.

No further noises followed.

Cursed old house.

After another minute of listening to silence passed, she crept toward the bedroom door. She gently placed her ear against the wood.

Still nothing.

She needed to keep her wits and not freak out.

With her breaths coming easier, she ducked into his bathroom where the contents of his medicine cabinet still sat on the vanity next to the sink. Earlier she'd looked only for ibuprofen, but she now took her time and read each label.

Still, no Viagra.

No sign of it anywhere else in the bathroom, either.

Where would a man like Albert Winthrop keep them? He'd obviously taken one the morning he'd died because she quite vividly recalled that his...member had remained stiff, even as he'd succumbed to death.

Hazel hadn't been with Florence for too long on that day before they'd heard the commotion. He had to have popped one not too much earlier than that, she'd guess.

An image of Mr. Winthrop hunched behind the wheel of his Mercedes as he forced her off the driveway flashed in her mind.

He'd been out somewhere prior to his time with Rachel and his following death. Maybe the pills were in his car?

Even if someone had poisoned his medication and that's what had killed him, that didn't mean it was Florence, she reasoned as she crept down the stairs, cringing when they creaked.

With no one in sight, she slipped out the front door undetected.

She crossed the drive to the large garage where Mr. Winthrop had kept multiple fancy cars. The side door opened easily, and she slipped right in.

Smells of grease and gasoline greeted her as she stepped farther into the darkened structure.

"Hello?" she called. While Mr. Winthrop had been alive, Mick Ramsey had spent a fair amount of time in this building and the one next door that housed the gardening tools. But as of late, he hadn't had much call to wash or fuel the cars for anyone's use.

She waited a few more seconds and then called again. "Mick, are you here?"

When she received no response, she strode toward the black Mercedes parked near the front of the garage.

The driver's door wasn't locked, so she opened it and sat on the seat. She checked the center console and gasped when she found the bottle of pills tucked away there. She really hadn't expected to be so lucky.

She pocketed them and stepped from the car.

"What do you think you're doing?" Mick appeared from between two cars and moved toward her in a way that left her on edge.

"I...was looking for Mrs. Winthrop's reading glasses."

He eyed her up and down in a very disrespectful and disgusting way. "Is that so? Did you find them?"

"No." She prayed the bottle of pills burning in her pocket didn't present too big of a bulge.

He snorted. "You honestly want me to believe that she asked you to look in a car that she's never once been in?"

Hazel went for the innocent shrug. "I've looked everywhere else."

"Uh-huh." He strode forward and grabbed her by the elbow.

She struggled to free herself, but his fingers dug deeper.

"I think you and me should go have a talk with the lady of the house right now, don't you? If she agrees, no problem. If not, I think she has the right to know she has a thief on her hands."

Hazel scrunched her features in disbelief as he jerked her toward the exit. "You think I was ransacking their vehicles, searching for...what?"

"Hard to tell what you might find in there. Mr. Winthrop always had cash if nothing else."

"This is ridiculous." She tried to jerk free again as they approached the front of the house. "You're hurting me."

"Just doing my job, protecting the property."

"You weren't hired to protect their property or watch Mr. Winthrop's private activities." She should have left Rachel out of it, but her anger had trumped her common sense.

"I see you've talked to Rachel. Friends, are you?" he leered at her. "Close friends, maybe? Witchy friends, even."

She punched at him with her free hand, but he caught it before she could do damage.

He pulled her inside the door, and pushed her to the hard, granite floor in the foyer. "Mrs. Jones," he hollered as he glared down at her.

A moment later, the woman appeared from the kitchen, and Hazel got to her feet. Her gaze jumped from Hazel to Mick. "What on earth is going on?"

"Found her ransacking the cars in the garage. Claims she was looking for Mrs. Winthrop's glasses."

"In the cars?" she asked Hazel with a puzzled look.

"I'd looked everywhere else," she repeated, knowing her answer wouldn't save her from damnation. She could only hope that Peter would rescue her once they called the police.

Mick snorted his disbelief. "Call the cops. I'll get Mrs. W. I think she'd like to know if this one has been taking advantage of her."

"Oh, come on," Hazel retorted. "If anyone would take advantage of her, it would be you."

Mrs. Jones shook her head in disappointment and headed toward the kitchen to call the police.

Hazel glared at Mick. "I wasn't looking to steal anything."

He smirked. "Then you have nothing to worry about."

"What on earth is all the yelling?" Florence appeared from the direction of the parlor and then widened her eyes when she spotted Hazel. "Hazel, dear. What are you doing here?"

Teddy came up behind her, surprising Hazel even more. Guilt and shame surely were written all over her face. Not for the reasons Mick expected, but it would be there all the same.

"I caught her in the garage trying to steal from you," Mick said before she could answer.

Hazel caught Florence's gaze and shook her head. "No."

Florence frowned and turned to her driver. "What is this nonsense that you're spouting, Mick?"

He cleared the dark hair from his eyes with a toss of his head. "Found this one rifling through Mr. Winthrop's Mercedes. She claims she was looking for your reading glasses."

"And?" Florence asked without missing a beat.

Hazel could scarcely breathe.

Mick's demeanor deflated. "Did you ask her to?"

"Yes."

The look on his face was beyond priceless. "*In the car?*"

She huffed impatiently. "I believe I just said yes. Do you have another concern?"

He took a step back. "No, ma'am."

"Then I'm sure you have better things to do than harass me and my dear friend."

"Yes, ma'am."

He departed, and Hazel wished she could have felt relieved. Florence eyed her for a long moment before she spoke.

"I know you, Hazel, and I know you wouldn't steal. So, would you care to tell me what exactly you were doing in Albert's car?"

CHAPTER NINETEEN

Hazel looked at Florence, and her heart broke. She flicked a glance at Teddy, not wanting to say anything in front of him, but she didn't seem to have a choice. "I don't want to tell you because you will hate me."

The poor, withered woman gave her a kind smile and held out her hand. "Of course, I won't hate you. Come and tell me so we can get past this nonsense and get back to being friends."

Hazel did as she asked and almost cried when Florence wrapped her cool fingers around her hand. Hazel squeezed and released a worried sigh. "I found something in your room earlier that troubled me. A pill. A blue pill."

Hazel paused to glance at Teddy for a reaction, but his expression remained the same.

"It wasn't one of your medications," Hazel continued. "So, I took it, and I asked...a friend if he knew what it was."

"I suspect he said Viagra," she responded.

"Yes," Hazel answered in surprise. She held tighter to the woman's hand. "Why would you have Viagra? You said you hadn't been close to Mr. Winthrop for quite some time."

She paused, not wanting to ask, but knowing she couldn't stop now. "Does it belong to Teddy?"

Teddy snorted. "I don't need Viagra."

Florence blushed but didn't glance at him. "No." She stared at the floor for several long moments and then turned to her friend and gave him a mournful smile. "I wish they were yours."

Teddy's eyebrows shot toward his hairline. "Florence? Why didn't you ever say anything? You know I would have taken you away from that bastard in a heartbeat."

Utter sadness consumed Florence's features. "I lost my chance for happiness a long time ago. If I would have left Albert for you, he would have made both our lives a living hell, and you deserved better."

"Better?" The word exploded from him. "This life I have is a shell of what it could have been with you in it. You know I have money, Florence. We could have moved somewhere else."

The older woman shook her head. "Wouldn't matter. He would have gone after your business, tried to hurt you or me any way that he could. He threatened me numerous times saying he would have been relentless. I believed him."

Hazel's stomach twisted into an aching knot, and she wished she could go back several hours and make a different choice after she'd noticed the pill. "So, the Viagra was Mr. Winthrop's then?" she asked quietly.

Slowly, Florence met Hazel's gaze. "Were the rest of them in his car?" she asked instead of answering.

Hazel nodded.

Florence gave a derisive snort. "I should have known. I only coated a couple of them with poison, so I wouldn't know when it was coming. I asked him to stop the affair. If he had, he'd still be here."

Her gaze teetered on the edge of reality. "He always kept them in his medicine cabinet, but after he died, they were gone. I searched this house from top to bottom. I thought maybe Rachel had taken them after...after...well, you know."

Tears welled in Hazel's eyes. "You poisoned him?"

She stared at her for a long time, and then her eyes filled with tears as well. She nodded. "He was an awful man, Hazel. I won't tell you the things he's done to me. But I married him, so I put up with them. But the day he publicly humiliated me in front of everyone, *in front of Teddy—*"

Teddy placed a comforting hand on her shoulder, and a sob escaped her. She covered her mouth with a shaking hand as though that would prevent another from doing the same.

But it didn't.

Teddy pulled her into his arms, and she released what must have been years of torment.

Florence had committed *murder.*

Hazel squeezed her eyes shut, knowing her dear elderly friend was going to jail, or at least she would receive some sort of punishment.

But Hazel couldn't find any anger in her heart toward her. Instead, she moved closer and placed a hand on the poor, abused woman's back. "Shh..." she whispered as anguish filled the room. "It's going to be okay."

"I couldn't take it anymore," Florence said between ragged breaths. "He bragged about the women he slept with. Told me all about Rachel, and how she was so pretty, and if I'd just take better care of myself. And then he'd hit me. And..." She broke off into another sob.

The doorbell rang, followed by several adamant knocks, startling Hazel but they didn't seem to faze Florence in the least. She was too lost in her grief.

Hazel opened the door to find Peter. Concern colored his features, and his right hand hovered on his hip near his gun.

"Hazel." He glanced beyond her. "Is everything okay?"

The heartbreak she'd absorbed combined with her own and overwhelmed her. She shook her head and stepped back to let him enter. "It was Florence. She's the one who poisoned her husband."

Peter's expression broke into sadness as he took in the scene. "I'm sorry," he whispered to Hazel. "I know she's your friend."

Without warning, he pulled her in for a hug.

Hazel knew she should push away, but she couldn't. Not yet. Not for a few more seconds. She needed someone to share her grief with as well.

"Are you here to arrest me?" Florence asked in a tear-stained voice.

Hazel slipped from Peter's embrace and moved to Florence's side.

Peter released a pained sigh. "The crime needs to be answered for. Even if you had a good reason."

Hazel patted her and did her best to absorb the grief pouring off her friend. "The chief is a good man. He will do what he can to help you."

Peter nodded in agreement.

"I'll be here for you, too," Teddy promised.

Tears streamed down her cheeks. "I know. Thank you. I don't deserve you all." She swiped shaking, fragile fingers across her face and sniffed. "Do you think we could wait a bit first?"

They all looked to the poor woman, waiting for an explanation.

"Could Hazel make me tea one last time, and we can sit here together for just a little while? For once, I would like to know what it's like to be free from him and free from carrying the burden of what I've done."

Peter didn't hesitate. "I don't see a problem with that."

Florence turned to Hazel with a questioning look.

"Of course." Hazel gave her a fierce hug. "Of course, we can. I'll have Mrs. Jones heat the water, and we'll chat like old friends for as long as you want."

Florence nodded with gratitude shimmering in her eyes. "Thank you."

Teddy wrapped an arm about her waist. "Let me help you into the parlor." Together, the two of them walked away, leaving Hazel alone with Peter.

Hazel dabbed at her tears. "Breaks my heart."

"Mine, too," Peter said and focused a closer gaze on her. "You okay?"

She ached to reach for him, to claim more of the comfort he'd offered her. But she couldn't. It wouldn't be right. "I'll be okay. I should probably get that tea made."

"Yeah." He glanced about the area as though making an assessment. "I have some things to take care of. How about I come back in a couple of hours. I'm not worried about Florence being a flight risk."

Her heart reached for him like she wished she could. "That's very kind."

He dipped his head in acknowledgement. "I'll see you in a while."

With that, he left, taking a piece of her heart with him.

EPILOGUE

"Hazel?" Gretta called from the front of the teashop. "Phone call."

Hazel had been so absorbed in her current tea creation, a blend of youthberry white tea and orange blossom herbal tea, that she hadn't heard the phone ring. She quickly scribbled where she'd stopped with the planned ingredients and headed out to the front of the store.

Gretta gave her a conspiratorial wink as she handed over the phone.

The wink gave it away, and she paused to steady her nerves. She hadn't talked to Peter for over a week. "Hello?"

"Hazel?" The rumble of Peter's sexy voice did that crazy thing to her stomach that it always did.

"Hello, Chief Parrish." She shot a narrow-eyed glare toward her smirking assistant.

"I wondered if you wanted to take a walk with me."

Blessed Mother, he knew exactly how to get to her. "Of course, we have plenty of that blend on the shelves."

"Same place as last time?"

"Sure. I don't mind bringing it over now. I know how much Margaret likes her tea, and you're very kind to think of her."

"Thirty minutes?"

"That should work. I'll just leave it with Margaret then."

He chuckled. "One of these days, you're going to have to give up the ghost, Hazel. People are smarter than you think."

Even though a retort burned on her tongue, she held the polite smile on her face. "Thanks again for calling. I appreciate your business." She hung up the phone without waiting for him to say goodbye.

If she couldn't argue with him, she could at least get the last word.

She placed the phone back under the counter and headed toward their stocked shelves in search of the tea she pretended she'd promised to deliver.

"Hot date?" Gretta called after her.

She rolled her eyes even though her assistant couldn't see her. She grabbed a tin of Majestic Mint and headed back to the counter. "I wish you all would stop trying to make something out of nothing. Chief Parrish is a nice man, but there's absolutely nothing between us."

Nothing but pure, old-fashioned, dangerous chemistry. "So, stop already."

"Mmm-hmm..." Gretta mumbled and grinned, but she wouldn't meet Hazel's gaze.

"It's almost four," Hazel said as she gathered her coat and scarf. "I think I'll knock off for the day after I drop this off. I need to return a book to the library, and the afternoon seems pretty slow."

"Sure thing, boss." Gretta snickered.

Finally, Hazel gave in and laughed. "Have fun with your fantasies. I'm going home."

The butterflies that had started when Peter had called increased with each pedal of her bike as she flew past the police station and continued down Main until she reached Vine Street, and then turned the corner onto Hemlock.

He stood, leaning against his car, looking amazing in jeans and boots. Her heart squeezed before thundering in her chest.

He smiled but said nothing as she passed him and headed toward the house, but she didn't miss the twinkle of interest burning in his eyes.

Her heart didn't stand a chance against him. Her only hope was that her brain could maintain control. She absolutely, one-hundred percent, could not let down her guard when she was around him. He liked the person he thought she was, she reminded herself for the millionth time.

Not who she really was.

She left her bike hidden behind the bushes and met him where the trees thickened into woods.

"Need my help again solving something?" she asked in a teasing voice.

He smiled, and the warmth of it shot straight into her soul. "I thought you might want to hear how Florence is doing."

She turned to him with a hopeful gaze. "Yes. Tell me."

"They have her under guard at an assisted living home in Boston for now until her sentencing. Sounds like the prosecution isn't interested in pressing full charges. I'd say it's not likely she'll come home anytime soon, but I was assured that they'll take pity on her and wherever she spends her time will likely be comfortable. Maybe a psych ward instead of jail."

That brought her a small measure of peace. Hazel knew her friend had to pay a penance for what she'd done, but she'd hoped the authorities would take her circumstances into consideration. "When you find out where she'll end up, will you let me know? I'd like to visit her. Take some tea if they'll let me."

"You betcha."

She grinned at his corny choice of words. "Hey, I wanted to tell you, too. I received an anonymous postcard, but I'm sure it's from Rachel. All it said was thanks and doing good."

Peter nodded. "Hopefully, she'll hear about Florence's arrest on the news and know that she's free from worry."

"I really hope so. She didn't deserve how people treated her."

"Yeah. I tried to give her the benefit of the doubt and act accordingly, but it was hard for her to see that in a town like this where others are not so forgiving."

She raised her brows and released a sigh, agreeing with his assessment.

He nudged her with his elbow. "On a happier note, I actually did have another case you might help me with."

"Oh, yeah? Not another murder, I hope."

"Nah, just a small mystery I'd like to solve. If you don't mind walking a bit, I'd like to pick that smart brain of yours."

"It is pretty smart," she teased. "But don't keep me out too late. The sun's going down, and it's already getting chilly."

"Deal," he said as their boots crunched the pinecones and twigs beneath their feet.

Warm fingers encircled hers, catching her off guard, sending her heart into a spiral. Sparks of electricity pierced her skin and warmed her entire body. Unsure what to do, she kept her gaze on the path ahead and tried to remember to breathe.

She should probably pull her hand from his, but she couldn't.

"This okay?" he asked after a few seconds.

Her brain screamed no, but her heart had control now. "Yes," she said quietly, and her emotions danced for joy.

He gave her hand a quick squeeze, drawing a smile to her lips. She might burn for this tomorrow, but right now, she didn't care.

When they were seated once again on a bench at the edge of the clearing, he turned to her. "Here's my dilemma. You tell me if you can figure out a way to solve it."

"Okay." She grinned. She'd always loved reading thrillers and playing mystery games. She was beginning to enjoy helping this man protect a town she'd grown to love. It gave her life purpose, and she knew she wanted to make this place her home.

If only she could know the people here would always love her the same. "Tell me."

He began giving her the details of someone in town who'd been deflating tires on seemingly random cars, and she found herself watching his lips as he talked. She doubted he needed her help on such a small case, but she liked that he'd used it as an excuse to see her.

There was much more she wanted to learn about her family's history, about Clarabelle and her book of spells. Perhaps even about Peter. She needed to figure out a way to access the special books at the library without creating suspicion, and she wanted to delve further into the incredible magic she'd discovered at the sacred grove.

In the meantime, she'd make sure she didn't fall into the same trap that had taken her ancestral grandmother from this earth. She'd watch her back, maintain her cover, and enjoy this beautiful town and all it had to offer.

Despite the dangers of living in Stonebridge, she admitted she wouldn't be leaving anytime soon. As much as she didn't belong, she knew in her heart she was right where she needed to be.

For now.

If you enjoyed reading this book, the greatest gift you can give me is to leave a short review at Amazon or Goodreads. It helps others find stories they might love and helps me find readers I might not otherwise. Your support means everything!

Thank you and happy reading,
Cindy

Excerpt from TWICE HEXED

Teas and Temptations Cozy Mystery Series
Book Two

Hazel Hardy hugged her jacket tighter around her as she hurried from her teashop along the cobblestone sidewalk of Main Street, small town Stonebridge, Massachusetts, to the cozy café down the block. The quaint town had enjoyed a very mild March, but as the month drew to a close, it seemed the Blessed Mother had changed her mind.

Ominous metal-gray clouds and a blustery wind warned of the high possibility of drenching rain. The weatherman said it would arrive some time that afternoon, which was why she'd decided to run to Cora's Café to make her delivery before the worst of the Nor'easter hit.

She neared the café door and caught a glimpse of a small sign tucked against the front window. It stated they proudly served Hazel's handcrafted teas, and she smiled. Her new partnership with Cora was working out very well. The town had accepted her as one of their own and many had gone out of their way to support her and her budding business.

If they knew the truth, that this same town had once persecuted her ancestral grandmother for being a witch, things would be much different. To this day, many of the prominent families in Stonebridge still feared and despised witches. If they discovered Hazel's identity, they'd likely run her out of town...or worse.

At least according to the police chief. And she had no reason to believe Chief Peter Parrish would exaggerate or lie.

Hazel gripped the café's doorknob and pulled, struggling to open the door against the strong winds. When she managed to get inside, the door pushed closed behind her as though warning her to take shelter and not leave until the storm had passed.

A few of the long-time residents sat in the old-fashioned eatery, enjoying the fried ham and scrambled egg special Cora always served on Tuesdays. A touch of cinnamon clung to the coffee-stained air, making her stomach growl.

"You had breakfast," she mumbled in return.

"Hazel," Cora called out from behind the counter and tucked a pencil into her blond, messy bun. Her smile was warm and welcoming as always, and it deepened the smile creases in her cheeks. By the time Cora was an old lady, the creases would likely be permanent wrinkles, but she'd be beautiful anyway.

Her friend deserted her spot behind the counter and approached. "You didn't have to come today. Not with the Witches' Wrath about to hit."

Hazel shrugged and pointed at the more-hardy citizens of Stonebridge. "If they're not worried, I'm not."

She hadn't experienced one of the town's epic storms yet, but she'd read about them in a book on the town's history that she'd borrowed from the library. Hazel wasn't sure if she believed what the author had written, but she claimed several of The Named, including Hazel's grandmother, had created the mother of all storms back in sixteen-ninety-something to punish the town during Ostara, the Spring Equinox.

The crazy storms had been happening this time of year ever since.

"The winds will knock over a few trees." The middle-aged Dotty Fingleton piped up from her seat in a nearby booth that she shared with her sister, June, and her teenaged daughter,

Sophie. The family's tree had roots growing back to a wealthy ship merchant who helped settle the town. "Then it'll dump some snow and be done, Cora. Same as always. I doubt it will be a big deal."

Before Hazel had learned otherwise, she never would have guessed Dotty and June were sisters. Dotty wore her bleached blond hair piled on top of her head giving her a sexy but disheveled look, and she preferred a younger-style of clothing.

June, on the other hand, embraced her age as far as clothing went. She kept her hair dyed red and closely cropped.

Dotty's daughter, Sophie, was a spitting image of her mother, thirty years younger, and probably just as much sass as her mother had had at that age.

Cora wiggled her pointer finger in contradiction. "Not a big deal? You're forgetting that one year when we got three feet of snow and it knocked the power out. We couldn't do anything for five days."

June nodded in agreement with Cora. "She's right. We all should be tucked safe in our homes long before two o'clock when they predict the storm will make a direct hit. I know I will be."

Dotty's daughter rolled her eyes, obviously used to her mother and aunt arguing.

"Whatever happened to your adventurous spirit?" Dotty asked as she lifted her coffee cup. "You've let old age steal it from you like we promised we never would."

June snorted and waved off her dig. "Oh, go eat worms. You don't know what you're talking about."

Hazel held back her grin, still not used to the old-fashioned, quirky phrases that many of the town's residents tossed out from time to time. Chief Parrish, the nightly star in her dreams and daily pain in her butt was one of the worst offenders. She wouldn't admit it to anyone, but sometimes those silly, odd words found their way straight to her heart.

Hazel lifted the large shopping bag, boasting her teashop's logo on the front, and set it on the counter. "Four large tins of Majestic Mint and another two of spiced chai."

Cora's eyes widened in excitement. "I hope this isn't eating into the customers who come into your store for tea and a chat."

Hazel shrugged and sent her a warm smile. "Not at all. Besides, as long as they're drinking my tea, I don't care where they're getting it."

"Spoken like a true businesswoman." Cora slipped around the side of the counter and tucked the tins below it. When she straightened, she had a small brown bakery box in her hands. "I've had another idea, too."

The contents of the box piqued her interest. "What do you have there?"

"Cookies," Cora said with enthusiasm shining in her eyes. "I wondered if you'd place these complimentary cookies in your shop. I had a few of these business cards printed that you could sit next to them. I hope to attract more of the summer visitors."

Hazel glanced at the cards that stated if they visited Cora's Café and presented the card, they could get another free one to take home for later, plus ten-percent off their café bill.

"That's so smart. One taste of your chocolate chip or snickerdoodle cookies, and you know they'll be in here begging for at least a dozen more. They'll probably stay for lunch or dinner, too."

Cora beamed. "That's what I'm hoping. I really need to cash in on the tourist season to keep my bottom line out of the red. Last year's sales weren't so great."

"Really?" She'd be so sad if Cora went out of business because she couldn't make ends meet, and she vowed to eat there more often.

The sound of a loud crash coming from outside snatched their attention.

June stood so she could see out the window. "There goes Elmer's sign, tumbling down the street."

Hazel's anxiety kicked up a notch. "Hope that doesn't happen to my store."

"Me, too. But at this point, all we can do is hope for the best and ride out the storm." She gave Hazel a carefree shrug. "Besides, Elmer's sign was barely hanging up as it was."

True. As soon as she left the café, she'd ask the Blessed Mother to protect them all.

With her worries slightly eased, another idea popped into Hazel's mind. "What if you bake cookies and brownies for me to sell in my shop? We can still do the complimentary cookie, but this way might catch those who don't intend to stay long enough to eat. Also, it will allow me to live up to the temptation part of Hazel's Teas and Temptations. Packaged cookies don't create frenzied desire like your cherry macaroons."

She ought to know. She'd eaten enough of them over the past few months.

Cora drew her brows together in thought as though she was working out the logistics of it. "I think that might actually work..."

Then Cora's face brightened. "Thanks, Hazel. You're the best. Have I mentioned that I'm super glad you moved here?"

"Only a thousand times, but I don't mind. I'm glad to be here, too."

She would continue to be happy as long as no one in town learned of the witch blood flowing through her veins. If they believed Hazel was what they termed a normal person, they'd be quite content to let her stay.

She shuddered to think of what might happen if anyone found out otherwise.

"So..." Cora said, dragging out the word. "How's Peter?"

Hazel wanted to groan in frustration, but that might encourage Cora's interest in her so-called love life. Instead, she pasted an innocent look on her face and leaned against the café's counter. "Chief Parrish? I don't know. Did something happen to him?"

"No." Cora's gaze turned sly. "I heard you two were dating."

She snorted. "Uh, that would be a negative. We are definitely not dating."

Not that she hadn't dreamt of it, but dating the town's chief who despised witches could only end in disaster. She'd caved to her emotions and held his hand one time, and now, she couldn't forget the feel of him. Dating would only make that worse.

The front door opened and slammed shut again, bringing with it a cold whip of blustery air.

Hazel, along with everyone else in the café, turned to the stranger who'd walked through the door. He unwound the scarf from his head to reveal a middle-aged, round face. A thick layer of scruff covered his chin, and he looked like he hadn't showered or combed his hair for days.

"Welcome to Cora's Café," Cora called. "Have a seat, and I'll be with you in a minute."

He lifted his chin in appreciation and smiled as he approached the counter. "Actually, I'm not in town for long. A coffee to go would be great. Throw in a muffin if you have one."

"You're planning to drive out of town right away?" Cora shot a glance at the clock over her shoulder. "You do realize you've picked a heck of a day to visit our little town. A big storm is looming on the horizon."

One of the older men sitting at the counter swiveled his gaze around, his bright blue eyes a contrast to his sallow and wrinkled skin. "Ought to listen to the lady," he warned.

Cora smiled at the older man before returning her gaze to the stranger. "You might reconsider renting a room at the motel because you'll likely be stuck here overnight."

"I've got four-wheel drive," the stranger said, his Jersey accent strong. "I'll be fine. Besides, my business here won't take long, and then I'll be back on the road."

Cora poured coffee in a to-go container. "Trust me. Unless you're prepared to be stranded on the road for a couple of days, you should get a room. You won't regret it."

He nodded but didn't verbalize his agreement, and Hazel suspected he wasn't a man who listened to reason. "I'm looking for Dotty Fingleton. I stopped by her house, and her housekeeper said I could find her here."

Dotty rotated her frosted-blond head around until she was looking at them over the back of her booth. "I'm Dotty Fingleton. Why would you be looking for me?"

The man cleared his throat and strode forward. The card he dug from his pocket and presented to her looked like it had ridden around in his jeans for quite some time. "Arnie James. Antique dealer out of Boston. I have a client who wanted me to contact you to see if you'd be interested in selling the King's Pearls."

Dotty dropped the card on the table and brought a hand to her throat. "The pearls? How could someone even know that I have them?"

"I can't discuss the details, but I'll just say I'm very good at what I do."

"Good at accosting women in public so you can take their jewels?" Her voice had risen several octaves.

"Dotty," her sister cautioned. "Don't let him upset you. The poor man hasn't accosted you. He only asked a question."

"Yeah, Mom," Sophie added, flicking her gaze between her mother and the man. "You don't have to freak out."

Dotty focused on her sister for a long moment and then released a large exhale. "Who exactly is this client who knows about my necklace?"

The stranger snorted. "Forgive me for saying so, but the location of the pearls given to your family by King William all those years ago isn't exactly black ops intelligence." The man puffed out his chest as he inhaled. "Specialized research led me in the right direction, followed by a few well-placed phone calls."

"You didn't answer my question." Dotty's voice had regained its nervous quality. "Who is your client?"

His half-hearted attempt at an apologetic smile failed. "My client wishes to remain anonymous."

"Then you can leave." Dotty jerked her thumb over her shoulder toward the front door.

He widened his eyes as though her response surprised him. "You haven't even heard my offer yet. Come on. It's five figures."

She eyed him with a cold stare. "I don't care what you're offering. Those pearls have been in my family for hundreds of years, and they will continue to stay that way. When I die, they will go to my daughter and then her daughter."

Sophie smiled smugly.

"Why?" His question held a whining quality. "You probably have them buried in a safe where no one ever sees them. What good are they there? Passed down from generation to generation like a burden that must be carried because the one before you did the same. Why don't you sell them to someone who really wants them? Someone who will take pleasure from them every day? You can take the money and buy yourself something nice."

Dotty snorted in disbelief. "Cora? Do you have this man's coffee and muffin ready? Because he's leaving."

Cora flicked a wide-eyed glance at Hazel, and she returned the gesture. "Coming right up."

The disappointed man headed toward the counter and paid for his food, but he stopped at their table again before leaving. "Call me if you change your mind."

Dotty turned her face from him. "Rest assured. I won't."

For several moments after the man had exited, no one in the café said a word.

Finally, Dotty released an exaggerated huff. "The nerve of some people."

"Right?" Sophie added. "Like he can just waltz in and take my inheritance from me?"

June shook her head. "I think you made a big deal out of nothing. He was only asking a question."

Just like that, the sisters were arguing again.

Cora watched them for a few seconds before turning her gaze to Hazel. "Nothing much changes around here."

Hazel grinned. "One of the things I love about Stonebridge."

Not long after, Hazel said her goodbyes, and she left with a package of Cora's amazing snickerdoodles and chocolate chip cookies tucked safely under her arm. As she forced open the door and stepped out, she smiled. She might be in for a heck of a storm, but she'd have no one in her store to eat the cookies.

She'd told Gretta to stay home, knowing business would be light and they'd be closing early, so Hazel wouldn't even have her assistant to help her devour them.

The Blessed Mother knew she wouldn't waste something so delicious.

If she couldn't eat them all, which was unlikely, she could freeze them for later.

She lowered her head against the blowing snow and headed down the cobblestone sidewalk toward her shop.

Several steps later, she barreled straight into a hard body.

You can find TWICE HEXED, Teas and Temptations Cozy Mystery Series, Book Two, on Amazon.com.

Book List

TEAS & TEMPTATIONS COZY MYSTERIES (PG-Rated Fun):
Once Wicked
Twice Hexed
Three Times Charmed
Four Warned
The Fifth Curse
It's All Sixes
Spellbound Seven
Elemental Eight
Nefarious Nine

BLACKWATER CANYON RANCH (Western Sexy Romance):
Caleb
Oliver
Justin
Piper
Jesse

ASPEN SERIES (Small Town Sexy Romance):
Wounded (Prequel)
Relentless
Lawless
Cowboys and Angels
Come Back to Me
Surrender
Reckless
Tempted
Crazy One More Time
I'm With You
Breathless

PINECONE VALLEY (Small Town Sexy Romance):
Love Me Again
Love Me Always

RETRIBUTION NOVELS (Sexy Romantic Suspense):
Branded
Hunted
Banished
Hijacked
Betrayed

ARGENT SPRINGS (Small Town Sexy Romance):
Whispers
Secrets

OTHER TITLES:
Moonlight and Margaritas (Sexy Contemporary Romance)
Sweet Vengeance (Sexy Romantic Suspense)

About the Author

Award-winning author Cindy Stark lives with her family and a sweet Border Collie in a small town shadowed by the Rocky Mountains. She writes fun, cozy witch mysteries, emotional romantic suspense, sexy contemporary romance. She loves to hear from readers!

Connect with her online at:
http://www.CindyStark.com
http://facebook.com/CindyStark19 (follow me)
https://www.facebook.com/cindy.stark.96780 (friend me)
https://www.amazon.com/Cindy-Stark/e/B008FT394W

Made in the USA
Middletown, DE
16 October 2023

40943917R00094